series « cinema-fictions » directed by

DANIÈLE RIVIÈRE

in the same series

RAUL RUIZ

Poetics of cinema, 1

Poetics of cinema, 2

The Book of Disappearances & The Book of Tractations

In Pursuit of Treasure Island

PETER GREENAWAY

Gold

The Falls

Rosa

Fear of Drowning by numbers

BRUNO DUMONT

Life of Jesus

Humanity

MANOEL DE OLIVEIRA

Angelica

Lisbonne Culturelle

Les Cannibales

1 cité Riverin
75010 Paris
France

www.disvoir.com

EAN 978-2-914563-72-7

RAOUL RUIZ

THE WIT OF THE STAIRCASE

Translated by Paul Buck & Catherine Petit

FIRST VIGIL

- *Is there a death after death?*

- *You won't believe me, but it's a popular joke in the Kingdom of Shadows.*

- *And is there a life after the cycle of so many lives and deaths? And are there illnesses, weaknesses, convalescences?*

- *I've told you already.*

And he laughed.

- *But I'm getting tired, Madame. Exhaustion exists, even for us...*

- *We'll stop the séance for today.*

Eight of the fourteen witnesses to the experiment hasten to leave. They go down the stairs. They talk in loud voices. They laugh a vulgar, sinister laugh. The other six stay for a while. They take little sips from a glass of cognac, and then leave the place, go down the stairs in silence, in a thick silence, loaded with an acid, frosty (those words are not mine) heaviness. All those movements, dispersed by draughts, can only awaken the spirit in the stairs. As for me, I stay.

But what me are we talking about?

"Me," meaning "the Belgian." Me, "the Belgian." As for me, I stay, and I think about bygone days.

- Do you remember, dear Arsène, my dearest Arsène, do you remember that memorable evening we became acquainted?

- Yes, a voice answers.

- But who are you, exactly? Here there is only me and myself.

- Yes, I remember you, my dear Flanders, that was your real name, wasn't it? Monsieur Flanders, Flanders the agathopède. What's new, Flanders? Any new invention? What silly thing inspired by the

Belgian spirit is haunting you at this very moment, in this communal night that makes us brothers?
- But I don't recognize you, my dear Arsène! That solemnity, that pomp…!
- I am searching for my voice…
- You!?
- Yes, Flanders. I haven't yet found my voice (from beyond the grave).
- For heaven's sake, Arsène, do wake up! It's eleven in the morning, we're facing each other in the Café de Valois. You probably ordered your usual hot chocolate with buttered bread and acacia honey, and you are exultant, for your dear friend Nerval has just been released! He has been declared sane by those from above. He could appear any moment now. But you no longer smile?… It seems to bother you…
- No, my Belgian friend, no. I am delighted. But I feel a kind of slight affliction at this moment which is curiously mixed, I have to admit, with the rejoicing that our dear Gérard's release naturally provokes within us. And all that gives rejoicing a bad taste. Are you following me?
- Not at all.
- I am at the same time pleased and not pleased.
- At the same time? You mean simultaneously?
- No, not that.

- *What do you think, Roland?*
- *Nothing, I think nothing of it.*
- *What about you, Paul?*
Paul remains silent.
Antoine sighs.
- *Failed. Yes, I would say it failed.*
- *I wouldn't be so peremptory. Madame Leblond is doing her best…*
- *In my opinion, she overdoes it.*
- *Cryptesthesy?*
- *You can call it what you want. She's making it up.*
- *But it's easy to check. The dates…*
- *Well, the dates…. That's easy…*
- *She cheats?*
- *We are cheating…*

They say “we”. What about me? I hear the whole conversation. I amble. I glide. I thread my way…. into Paul’s nose, into Antoine’s ears…

- *Failed? I wouldn’t go as far as that.*
- *Well, next time…*
- *I’m afraid there won’t be any next time.*
- *We’ll see, we’ll see!*

We’ll see. You’ll call me and I shall come. What am I saying? Me, come? It has been a while since I’ve moved from here. But what’s bothering me is the sloppiness of the place.

Here? What is it, “here”? What is that stillness?

I have to admit I cannot see a thing. Shadows. That famous greyness that we spoke about at the time. What time? Let’s see. The memories, here. To make the past return.

But first, what past?

Well, to tell you the truth, there are always two things that come to mind when I only invited one. Let’s say I want to make my first communion come back. Well, sometimes it’s accompanied by my mother’s funeral.

The memories set in, of course, a bit like a tableau vivant. Everything is there: a certain stillness, or rather, suspension.

I see myself (a way of speaking: the greyness accommodates my memories the best it can). He is here, the little darling (me). But what are those half-naked female dancers doing here? And what about that lame donkey walking around its erection? And even worse, why that hussar who finds it very hard to stand up? And those voices in the background, shouting “Long live the Emperor!”

That’s it, memories get all mixed up in a soup that stinks of onion. Yes, smells exist. It’s thanks to the smells that one manages to see. The smells precede the visions (always two tableaux that one finds it very hard to make out). Toast brings about the apparition of the ride of the headless men (a way of speaking), the scent of violets always brings forth the flying sailing boats. Processions are often heralded by the irritating presence of an aroma of boiled beef. And with the sounds of bells, all images are corroded by a crepuscular red.

Indeed, memories set in around me. But one should point out that there is a place for each thing. There is especially a place for each of the parts of “the in-between-me”, as I call this life. This survival.

My "in-between-me" finds its place in a damp hollow (a dampness of wet dog), in that place that a poor tramp called Soap uses as a shelter. It is at his place I settle. It is my kingdom, the temple of bygone things. Each time I feel the desire to relive my past, I settle there to invoke the shadows of old. When I say "the shadows of old", do not think I'm using a metaphor, certainly not. When I call the things and people of the past, it is the shadows that settle themselves first. Through the intermediary of odours, they invite the bright images of my past. Of course there is another past, the one I call "the intruder past", if I can call it that. After my death, I took care to conserve my syntactical peculiarities, my awkward adjectives. Isn't it odd that I never tried since that vague death of mine, to learn Flemish, my mother tongue, even less German, my mother's tongue, or even English, my second language?

That's how it is. In that vaguely sad, opaque beyond which is mine, there is only French. It is the language from beyond the grave. And I have to say to you (you? who, you?) I had to witness arguments between scholars and philistines in a French that would make an Ethiopian slave blush, a dove (normally sane) crazy. Indeed, all those gentle folk were speaking in a French that would make the hair stand on end on the skull of a bald Cistercian!

- *Another cognac?*

- *No, not for me, thank you.*

- *For me neither, it's getting late. Today I'm invited to have dinner at Camille's, with a group of British decadents.*

- *Burton?*

- *No, not him.*

- *He's not well, I'm told.*

I have to admit I am cheating, or almost. Memories don't come just like that. I think I mentioned it already. First, there are the colours. In this case, it's more like yellow. And the smell of coffee. And the anti-chronies, those events that tickle things, upset their course… perhaps I should call them chronics?

- But tell me, my friend! Tell me, what about your friends? The agathopèdes?

- It's been a while since I last saw them. I have to say I travel quite a lot, these days. Belgium, you know? Belgium is far away.

- Yes, I've been told.

- Well, to be honest… the agathopèdes have never really been my cup of tea.

- Really? How's that? I've been told you have a new project!

- Memories from beyond the grave? That's an old one!

- *Your* memories from beyond the grave.

- Yes, it was that.

- I was also told you had contacted a horde of spiritualists. They supposedly pretend to summon you, and to make it all implausible, you would have finagled into having a first class funeral. In Ghent, or am I mistaken?

- Oh, one hears so many things.

- I was most definitely told you were in the coffin, as one could say *corpore praesenti*.

- Let's say it's true. I've always liked coffins. At a certain period in my life, I didn't miss a single funeral. Funerals were my thing. Yes, let's say that. So what? That doesn't mean the whole story is true, does it? Even though it's plausible!

- At least it means all that is in the spirit of your friends the agathopèdes. Of their poetics, in a way.

- But you talk about the agathopèdes as if they existed. As if they were a sect or a political party!

- A club, perhaps?

- Not even that. Did you know we never actually got together? There never was a general assembly, not even a dinner at *La Main qui parle*. All of that is simply not true.

- You've been seen!

- What does that prove? Chance exists!

- No, my Belgian friend, chance does not exist.

Of course. But there had never been anything else but chance. I have never seen, neither from close nor from afar, one single agathopède. Or rather… there was actually a group of friends. Pranksters. A few English, a few Italians, and even a South-American. And what do pranksters do? Pranks, that's all. So there was one. Someone started to talk about a non-existent book: *The depravity of the prophet.* We talked about it, and talked about it some more, and by talking each evening about that famous *Depravity*, we ended up believing we had actually read it. And what could we possibly do with that book once we had all read it? We wrote it; that's it.

- And what was the subject of the book?

- Well, me. As simple as that! The man buried alive.

Yes, at that moment (but what exactly is a moment?), at that very moment, I see myself surrounded by men in black. They hadn't chosen the right cemetery, it's true. No witnesses, no visitors. Or rather only indifferent witnesses. However, I was there. In the coffin. I was in there. And I was suffocating!

I can see the whole scene once more. Preceded, like you might expect, by the disturbing fragrance of wild strawberries. And adorned with a nursery rhyme from Alsace. The whole thing tinged with a cardinal red.

Do I have to clarify that the prank turned out badly? That I was found dead when the coffin was reopened?

Dead from suffocation. That's it.

Suddenly, here I am, back at the Café de Valois.

Gérard has just made an appearance.

Everyone pretends not to notice him. Which he enjoys. As always, he is smiling, overburdened by that sad smile that keeps you at a distance.

- Is it you, Gérard?! I didn't recognize you. You've lost weight.

- Me? No. It's the other who takes it all. It's my other who fattens up.

- Dear Gérard! He hasn't changed. Always on form!

He sits at his usual place. I come closer. He looks at me, still smiling. He shakes my hand, and now he slips in it (in my hand!) a grubby, sodden ball of paper on which he had probably chewed and then carried in his pocket for days!

- It's for you, he says. It's for you. I must confess it was not destined for you. At the beginning, I first thought of Saint-Hilaire. He is the only one who could be interested, even fascinated by this amazing thing. This egg, you see, this egg has already travelled across four countries. First yours, your beloved Belgium, then Holland, Germany and, of course, Ethiopia. You know what I'm taking about. This egg, I'm telling you in confidence, this egg is on the point of giving birth to a rare bird. *Rara avis*. Not really a bird, however. I'd rather say a porcupine, tiny but decorated with wings, enough to break your heart.

I look at the papier-mâché egg. Homemade. I look at Gérard's hands. They don't stop. They move, they flutter like a suffocating heart. Like my own heart in the agathopède coffin.

- I see, Gérard. And I'm extremely grateful to you for having entrusted me with that mission. I intend to bring it to a successful conclusion.

- Above all, don't forget our Ethiopian friends, they are waiting for some news.

- I most certainly won't, my dear Gérard.

On that note he leaves, without saying goodbye, and I stay there with the plump egg in my hand.

But... what's happening? The egg quivers! This egg is alive! I must show it straight away to Saint-Hilaire! The egg is alive!

At that moment, I notice all the fellows in the Café de Valois are staring at me.

A waiter with a white apron approaches.

- You shouldn't have laughed, sir.

I look at him, dumbfounded.

- But I didn't laugh.

- You had a little smile, yes. You shouldn't.

- But Gaston, I know very well that Gérard was speaking perfectly seriously when he suggested I bring that ball to Monsieur de Saint-Hilaire. And I have every intention to do so as early as this afternoon.

- A little smile, nevertheless. He was offended.

- You are making that up, Gaston!

- I won't insist, but nevertheless, you shouldn't have smiled...

- I admit, I could have smiled a little without meaning to, it happens quite often. But I didn't make fun of him, not at all!

- That's true, Gaston, a customer seated near the window exclaims, you're trying too hard to be a good fellow.

- Certainly not, I'm warning you.

- I am the one who's warning you!

They both stand, the thing turns sour.

- Come on, come on, dear friends, the owner intervenes, keep calm!

- But I'm very calm, the customer protests.

He keeps quiet, or rather is interrupted by a large cobblestone coming straight from the rue de Valois that shatters the window.

- That was bound to happen! That is just like Gérard, the owner points out, bringing out his ledger.

He takes note, out loud, “one broken window: 40 francs”.

Gérard reappears, grabs three or four coffee cups and hurls them to the back of the room.

The owner announces, writing it all down: “four coffee cups, a jar, a broken chair: 18 francs”.

The customers immediately start emptying their pockets. The collection of the kitty is done with utmost discretion.

After a good ten minutes of these shenanigans, almost half of the crowd in the café is already incapacitated.

Gérard is still smiling.

In vain a few courageous customers try to calm him.

- We don’t want the police to interfere, a customer warns, promptly receiving a coffee pot full in the face.

And the scene lasts until a good mood takes over. In the end, everybody is laughing heartily.

Gérard sees me and comes across.

- You were the only one, he says, the only one who was right!

And he embraces me. Then he disappears, singing an air from the Valois, his beloved country.

Yes, I can clearly see that scene, which smells of cardamom, and stinks of navy blue. Then a voice puts an end to those outlandish rambles. The song, the same song, coming from the Valois. Nerval’s song.

It is Soap, the tramp, who has come to sleep. Today he’s early.

And he talks to me. Yes, the tramp talks to me.

- Are you there, my good man?

I cannot respond, I have no voice. But he knows I’m here.

- Are you there, spirit of the staircase?

That’s what he calls me: spirit of the staircase.

- First, I have to tell you something: your pals, the spiritualists, they don’t get it. Nothing at all. They moan, thinking a spirit must be spiritual. Must speak with spirit, if you like. See what I mean. They think you speak with a dull gravity. Dull! Can you imagine? They say that exactly with a very grave tone… and a very dull one too. If you want my opinion, don’t answer when they call! Tell them to go to h… Well, you get my meaning.

How does he do it, how does he know I'm here? How can he tell when I'm not even sure I'm here? It's time for everyone to know: I have the greatest difficulty adapting to those centripetal whirlwinds, to those viscous apnoea that surround me and that I call, for lack of a better expression, "my very own little space". Nothing less plausible than that manner of speaking: no little space, no home. All that is nothing but a hazy landscape. I may as well say "mountain", or "far away sea", "Parisian greyness" or even talk about a fog enveloping everything in an eternal drizzle. "Eternal"? No, not even that. Let everyone know: here, nothing is eternal. In that slimy thickness, one manages the best one can, between the dreadful tremor of the ephemeral crowd of those "almost souls" and the emphatic barrenness of the wanderers. Oh dear Lord! And I get lost in the endless discussions that fill the beyond the grave. This beyond the grave, I mean, for there are others. I haven't faced them yet, but I can feel their presence. In the end, there's nothing but bad weather. And with all that bric-à-brac, those broken tools, what can one do? Go into antiques, that's it! A trade with a future (yes, my friends, on the other hand, the future exists, one could even say it's the only thing that does exist!).

- You shouldn't be at their beck and call, do you get it? Soap repeats.

He looks around him, as if lost. He takes a last sip and he's off.

I remain on the spot, exhausted. Yes, that's the right word. In this world of "semi-darkness", there is nothing else: a life sentence of exhaustion, one could say.

SECOND VIGIL

- *Is there anybody there?*
- *Yes, there is: me, but I abstain.*
- *Anybody there?*

The ouija board is ready. Everything is ready. I occupy the place. Without rushing. My shadows settle here and there.

- *Surname, first name.*
- *Flanders Karl August, known as "The Belgian".*
- *Date of birth?*
- *Ghent, 18 September 1810.*
- *Is Flanders your real name?*
- *Yes.*
- *Profession?*
- *Agathopède.*
- *What on earth is that?*
- *A profession like any other.*
- *Do you make a living from it?*
- *Yes, it's possible.*
- *Explain.*
- *It's impossible to explain.*
- *What do you do, precisely?*
- *In the world of the agathopèdes, nothing specific.*
- *And you call that a profession!*
- *One takes it on, one does it, one earns a living.*
- *Do you earn much?*
- *Not much. Or much too much. In the end, it's worth it.*
- *In the end?*
- *We make pranks. Long-term pranks. A prank is like a time bomb.*

It needs time.

- How much time?

- Sometimes a hundred years.

- That means some of those bombs haven't exploded yet?

- There is one exploding at this very moment.

- Explain.

- No. It doesn't amuse me to do so.

Silence.

- We'll terminate the séance.

The fourteen members of the society rise. Nine leave, the remaining five head for the lounge. Antoine pours five glasses of cognac. No one talks. The wind can be heard whistling.

- It's going to rain.

- Yes, it looks like it.

- I have to go. I'm expected.

- Wait a minute. I have something to tell you. Something that could turn everything upside down.

- Really? I'm interested... What is it?

- A photographer.

- Ah, that one! I've heard about him already. It's that dear old Gamay, isn't it?

- The one who claims it's possible to take photos of ghosts?

- He's done it already!

- I heard that. I also heard he spent a few months in Sainte-Anne.

- He's not mad.

- Let's leave it at that! And when will he be there?

- Next week.

- I'm not sure I can come. And to be honest, I don't believe in it. I've seen the photos, you can't really see anything.

They leave in a hurry, like typical Parisians. One of them leafs through his diary and pretends to be in a panic.

- Oh my God! I'm not sure I'll be there on time, with that traffic congestion!

It takes all sorts!

I go back to the alcove under the stairs and do my best to stick the pieces back together. To stick back together my astral body, that I'm tempted to call "cloacal" (another Belgian French expression). My leg hurts. Humidity doesn't suit the greyness of my body. It was Gautier, I believe, who used to talk about "abstract" pains to convey the atrocity of the toothache that sometimes plagued him at the end of an overly long winter.

"I feel an abstract pain, he would say. Out of place with the neuralgic zone, I mean."

Pains? Yes, they exist even after that temporary death.

My leg hurts, and that ache is in the process of shifting painfully towards one of the stairs, from where the spirit has the honour of telling you those few words from beyond the grave.

But beyond which grave, by the way? I was pushed into the bottomless well. The communal grave! There lies my former body. And I rejoice from visiting it now and then.

It is no longer there. But I am. I am well and truly there. I pay it a visit every Friday. Before my photo sittings. Yes, those are part of my so-called "spiritual" activities. Hence, listening to my spiritualists talking about a photographer makes me laugh. Oh yes, what a laugh I'm having! I know very well, only too well, what a sitting really means. And I take that very seriously. Théodule d'Antibes takes photographs from beyond the grave, that's correct. They are even very good. He knows how to handle those figures that shiver in the fog. He is gifted, there's no doubt about that. To start with, he is a medium, a real one. He never fails, he knows the music. "To each his ghost," he says. And he believes it.

During my last sitting, he was not alone. There was someone else. A specimen with an overly piercing eye, who almost made the whole "operation" fail. That is how Antibes calls our sittings. For him they are "operations", in the way one speaks about surgical interventions.

- May I introduce you to Monsieur Farigoule. He will be present today. He is very keen on it, being one of us. He is the author of an essay on "the extra-retinal vision and the paroptic sense".

I arrange my clouds the best I can.

- He is here, says Théodule.

- I can see, says Farigoule, his eyes closed tight.

Théodule sets up his system (I am present, I see everything through his eyes). Farigoule covers his head with a kind of mask or shoebox.

He is stripped to the waist.

- I'm ready, he says.

He looks at me, I can feel it. He looks at me with the countless eyes of his chest.

- I'm ready!

- Be a bit patient! says Théodule. Nothing is easy with these type of things! It's not called "the beyond" for nothing.

- It's not the beyond I'm interested in, obviously! It's what's going to happen here.

Théodule doesn't reply. He is busy preparing his instruments: a hermetic box inside which twenty or so mirrors, whose mechanisms have been adjusted to within a millimetre, produce the sound of a clock.

- I'm almost done.

And then, turning his body to the left, to the right, then slightly backwards, forwards... :

- There we are. We can start.

The shutters are pulled, the semi-dark is ours. The semi-dark... Not just any, that semi-dark he uses as lighting.

- I see something like... I don't know... a sand storm, Farigoule exclaims.

- We're not far from it, whispers Théodule.

- There we are! The famous whirlwind. We have it!

Ah! How painful it all is! But there is no better remedy for the pains of ghostly legs.

- Strike a pose, my friend. Come on!

Well, that is Théodule's great discovery: ghosts have to strike poses. Failing that, no photographs.

I comply.

- Ah no, no, not like that! A more nonchalant pose. You need to simulate stillness, that's all. Have a rest first, then portray that rest.

Rest? What rest? It doesn't exist! Fatigue, yes. Aching legs, nausea, everything you wish, but rest...

- Come on, my dear, one has to get used to it! It has never been easy, remember the last sitting! All that is gruelling for you, of course, but it's the same for me.

His voice reaches me from a distance. On the contrary, it seems that

Farigoule's voice is coming out of me, that it is not even a voice, but something like a song with no words.

Théodule is getting annoyed.

- What on earth is happening today! Today of all days! You disappoint me, Flanders! Maria was ten times more focused. At least she knows what striking a pose means.

He starts to insult me.

- Keep calm, Farigoule tries to restrain him. Science needs patience.

- I don't care about science, I want my photographs!

He adds a black curtain. And another. Then yet another.

The semi-dark is blinding.

And suddenly I feel my body "coming back" to me. I can feel my two legs (two, not three). My head puts up with a heaviness that startles me. My arms move about.

I am here. With my whole body!

I enter directly into the other world, the one of the dying.

The room is bathed in a silvery fuzziness. The back of the room is lit then becomes dark in an illogical way. Everything has the polish of agate. There is something impossible, a delirious tremor touches the surface of the scene. And at the back of the studio, there is someone who strikes poses.

- That's perfect, Théodule says, there you are, I recognise you now, my old friend.

Suddenly, something happens. I see neither through Théodule's eyes nor through Farigoule's chest. I see, that's all. Without a viewpoint. My eye glides without stopping. Rather well. It swims. My eye is a fish. I envelop the whole room. My vision hurts. I have a pain that doesn't escape through the sole eye.

I see like I used to. Like I've never seen before, to be honest.

- Ah, I see him, Farigoule says. He is here.

Yes, I'm here. I see myself surrounded with things seen in bygone days...

I am at Devéria's. That good Eugène is busily putting the finishing touches to his masterpiece: *The Birth of Henry IV*. Therefore we must be in 1827. I am seventeen years old. I've just arrived in Paris. Only a few days ago I was introduced to the world of the Devérias and Eugène took me under his wing.

He was young, twenty-two years old, and was about to become

famous a few weeks later. I can see myself, I can see him. Me as a young model, and him, smiling and warm. He has seen all sorts, dear old Eugène.

The few guests are keeping a reverential silence or whisper fitting comments.

- He will be talked about.

- He is already talked about.

One of them takes me by the arm.

- So you are the young, talented and promising one? Is it you, Flanders?

- Yes, it is me.

- I am Flers, Camille Flers. Eugène begged me to give you a few lessons. I'll expect you tomorrow at dawn. We'll go around Aumale, and you will see. You too will learn to make a big thing out of frogs' croaks. There frogs croak all day. There are several tribes, if I may say. One has to let oneself be guided by the music. And be very attentive. When the frogs stop croaking, that's the place one should settle! When you understand that, you will understand everything. I expect you at my house. At dawn. Here's my address. My barouche will be waiting for you. I'll be there.

My daydreaming is interrupted: there's a knock on Théodule's door.

- Eh! Are you going to stop your experiments? It's leaking!

- What do you mean, it's leaking?

- Come and see! It's dripping. Come. The ceiling is ruined!

- Yes, all of this is not only spiritual... There's also matter. And it stinks!

- It smells like sulphur.

Farigoule gets dressed.

- We need to go over that calmly.

- Yes, we need to.

- Anyway, it was very interesting.

- Did you enjoy it?

- Every second was stimulating! I would go as far as to say that it was very exciting.

- I'm delighted.

- Me too. Keep in touch.

He leaves.

Théodule remains alone. He ambles, walks up and down, exclaims "too much is too much!" and leaves by the door.

I remain alone in the place.

Alone? Not entirely.

There are others. Four? Five? Perhaps more. Much more. A crowd of half-visible revenants.

We go round and round.

When I cross paths with one of them, I mean a semi-visible presence, I'm surprised to notice how dressed up they all are. I say "dressed up", as one is dressed to go to a party. Here comes one, and he is only one example, Revard, the painter with four hands: his morning coat flared at the shoulder displays large velvet lapels and reveals his bulging chest under a waistcoat shaped as a pourpoint. He parades around, his eyes closed. All his fellows are sporting appropriate black clothes. A few evanescent ladies also appear, the scarlet and the persistent smell of eucalyptus making them even more spiritual than they are naturally.

There are the "others", Théodule's models. In a few weeks time, he intends to present his exhibition in galleries for amazing arts: a choice of his beyond the grave images. Poor Théodule, he was born too early... Today, he would be a sensation. I can see him, anxious-looking, his eyes shifty but attentive. The press proclaimed this morning: "Théodule d'Antibes will shortly unveil images of his travels in the seventh continent!" It will be, without doubt, the "exhibition of the century". And here are the first guests rushing forth, looking sceptical:

- The "antiboscope", you were saying? What is it exactly, an antiboscope?

- Surely you must know? It is Monsieur d'Antibes' latest invention! That dear Théodule will never cease to amaze us.

- I heard one sees in them the truth of the afterlife.

- The afterlife? The beyond, you mean!

- He succeeded in showing dead fellows.

- Is that it? And where did he find them? In the cemetery?

- It's a very well-kept secret...

- Look, Madame Dorval has arrived. It's not going to be long now.

And I see you, my dear Théodule. You are there, in front of the open door to the great hall. One can make out very large frames, one barely sees them for they are concealed. You had a rather complex system of velvet curtains arranged. They are all going to fall at the same time.

That's it, done.

A huge silence.

A silence difficult to describe. That wrings your heart. Suffocates you.

A lady faints, then another and still another.

- Stop, too much is too much!

There are good reasons to be moved, it's true.

It's not only due to the presence of the dead. We've seen all sorts. The daguerrotypes have already shown us deceased men and women. Like the victims of the plague, to mention a few. But those dead fellows, they are alive!

Perhaps at that very moment they are even here, among us. It's death given back to the present.

No, it's not only due to the unbearable vision of those ghosts who "pose", nor even to the fact that they take outlandish, almost obscene poses. It's due to their gaze! It pierces you to the quick, if I may say so. It strips you naked.

- But it's Graziano! More himself than his real self! And here is Philothée O'Neddy!

Yes, Théodule, it could have been a huge success. Alas, people were not ready yet.

All my colleagues (what else to call them?), all my colleagues disperse, swallowed by draughts. I take the opportunity to slip away too. I float and dissolve into the Parisian greyness.

Here I am again, under the stairs.

- Ah, there you are, at last!

He must have been waiting for me, my old tramp! But how does he always know when I'm there? Sometimes it even seems he guesses and follows my thoughts. An impossible thing, surely, as one knows, for I have no inside. I mean to say that thing… thought… I don't have it inside me. In its place, there's a roughness of the mind. Onion peels, at most, corresponding to feelings. Well, something of that ilk.

- Yes, I understand you, he says, I'm like you, I let myself go, I float in the air.

There's no doubt: he listens to me and understands me.

THIRD VIGIL

- Tonight, there will be a photographer among us, we hope it is not going to disturb you too much.

- I'm used to it.

- Really? How's that? In your day, there were not yet photographers!

- In the forties, it was very fashionable.

- Oh yes, the daguerreotype! Today we've developed new techniques. We can reach up to you.

- I'm used to it.

The photographer is setting up his lights. And already he makes a mistake: there is too much light. Much too much. And the colour of the projectors is wrong.

- While we're waiting, tell us about your childhood.

- My childhood? That's the future.

- Yes, all right, and so?

- That's all.

- Why the future?

- Because it hasn't happened yet.

- A manner of speaking, surely.

- If you wish...

- Come on, an image... An image of your childhood.

- A kite.

- That's it, better than nothing!

- But it hasn't happened yet. It will happen in a few week's time.

- I'm not quite with you.

- Childhood, you know. Childhood here is scattered. Like everything, in fact. Childhood is a mosaic. It's nothing but a whim, it swirls around. A kite here, a frantic race there, dust, more dust, still more dust. And then, suddenly, a clock that hums. And a ride. Let's not forget, of course, the visited house.

- *The visited house?*

- *It was much spoken about. And it will be spoken about again. It was simply an un-inhabited house, a kind of hotel used as a shelter by pilgrim- phantoms. You know, don't you, like migrating birds, phantoms travel. That said, even in the greyness, everything is well-ordered. In that desolate twilight meander pre-established paths that one is forced to follow. And that is how we go round and round. Well, them, I mean the others. Personally I found myself a home, under the staircase.*

- *And that visited house, it belongs to your childhood?*

- *Yes, to my childhood long ago. I can see it, engulfed by sand.*

- *Where's that?*

- *Ostend. With my family.*

- *Tell us about your family.*

But the photographer's light shatters the room into a thousand pieces.

I find myself elsewhere, a thousand kilometres away.

On a beach. Oh, it's Ostend.

I can see my grand-mother, my Uncle Julius. They are looking at a shell that has come from elsewhere.

- Never seen anything like it! says my uncle.

- It reminds me of something, my grandmother whispers.

In the distance one can see four beguines running, unnerved by the Ostend wind.

The visited house is there. Our second residence. Second? Not sure. I would rather say the mobile house. Yes, members of my family had that gypsy aspect. They had conceived a transportable house. When we felt like it, we fitted wheels and took to the road for a change of air. In fact, the visited house was also a house on a visit. It made itself invited whenever it saw fit. Agathopedy was already in the air!

But how could they have built such a house? Julius had said it was already old. That his grandfather had claimed that manner of building houses had come from beyond the sea. The story goes that a boat had been shipwrecked before Ostend. The survivors had settled in the area. They had built several houses, four or five. Or even more. And all those houses had the particularity that "they were transportable". Those shipwreck survivors were quick-tempered, rowdy, and difficult. And when they argued between themselves, they took their house and left for a change of air. At the time it was possible, the authorities used to close their eyes. But later on everything became more complicated. First, there were wars. Listen, without going any further: at Waterloo, it seems that one of those houses went right across the battlefield, drawn by thirty or more oxen, without the occupants deeming it necessary to leave the dining room in which they were quietly enjoying a Flemish-style cassoulet.

In the visited house, it goes without saying, there was no lack of draughts. Contradictory draughts. So we made the most of it by flying kites of all different colours in the rooms. Tiny kites for indoor use. There already was something agathopedic in that too. Yes, we were all eccentrics "from beyond the sea". Julius the first.

He was learned, as one says. Had a "doctorate in Theology" from Leuven. A great mind, he was involved in a violent quarrel, and in the end was expelled from the University. Rumour has it that he was seduced by a group of preadamite troublemakers. Radicals. They had resuscitated a sect one thought well and truly dead. They claimed that before Adam the earth was populated with men and women just like you and me. Wretched people, troglodytes in a way. In their eyes, Monsieur Adam and Madame Eve were nothing but the despicable elected. The favourites. Spoilt children. Can you imagine? And then, as is often the case, there were dissidents. A man named Futrus, or Gutrus, developed a strange conception, that he called "the minor essenism": those preadamite creatures had created themselves, imitating God, and following a process as questionable as self-production, that he called in the aftermath "self-degenerative collisions". Seen from afar, all those quarrels appear to be slightly ridiculous, if not pathetic. But our uncle was blamed, expelled and banished. His fellow students avoided him. In a student café, he was refused a table. Even worse, no doctor agreed to treat the rabies he contracted one evening, when he was bitten by a dog. He should have died, but he pulled through all by himself, after what he called his "fight with the angel". Having come from beyond the sea, his ancestors landed one evening, and came to his rescue. One day, he appeared at our door. He avoided people, stared at the tip of his shoes, and smiled with a smile that came from far away. Every day at dusk, he used to go for a walk. He hummed to himself and communicated, one says, a "dark rejoicing".

My grandmother told me all that.

- Your uncle was not alone. He was "surrounded". He was "visited". He had made a pact. No doubt about that! He had signed. Do you know how to recognise someone who has signed? You just need to look at the forefinger. There's always a tiny pinprick of blood. Barely visible. Your uncle was sucking that finger. Day and night. And he used to mumble words from afar. From beyond the sea.

- He had made a pact?

- We were never entirely sure. He already had that strange habit of venerating shells. And do you know how to also recognise the one who has definitely taken a commitment? That person is never alone. There is always someone near him, a stray dog, a seagull, a cat... But more important still, the "ben andanti" recognised him as one of them. They called your uncle, brother. They made him gifts. One gift in particular. One. A black hen, whose throat your uncle used to cut at midnight. Always at midnight. He was surrounded, that's for sure. Around him he had a crowd of shadows. It was visible at night. You know, when one roasts chestnuts in the grate... You know? Well, on the wall, one could often see shadows coming from nowhere. Visiting shadows.

A chatterbox, that's my grandmother.

And the most curious was that your uncle, your old uncle, was listening to all those gossips, quietly sucking his forefinger. He listened to everything, and smiled. He was examining the shell. With a sailor's magnifying glass. One evening, he said to me:

- Come closer, boy, come, have a look!

He showed me the thing. I saw a dance. I heard screams that shattered me. One couldn't see much. A faraway island. Birds sniggering, chilling your blood.

- Did you see? Did you hear? Now look at the wall.

And I saw the shadows the grandmother talked about. The shadows coming from nowhere.

We lived alone, there, in Ostend. As for our family, we had news through a cousin of mine, married to a fisherman. Cunégonde was very young. She loved her husband. She often used to go to Ghent. To the market. And she sometimes met my mother and my sisters. As for my father, he was never there. He officially lived in England, where he had a second family. My sisters left one after another for the convent, where they were taught strange skills. I didn't understand much. But I never asked questions. Things happened, that was all. I was quite happy to do nothing. Nothing or not much. Father Audiard gave me lessons. I learned to read and write in Flemish and German. My father wrote me letters in English and sometimes my sisters added drawings of nameless flowers. They did it on purpose to insist on the un-nameable aspect of those flowers. They were not exactly flowers. They were vegetal animals. They walked. I even remember one of them, scarlet, with a little suitcase in its hand. They were funny, my sisters from the other side of the Channel. So I sent them flying boats, sometimes in flames. My uncle, the bewitched, had assured me that at the preadamite time, boats were flying and often burst into flames. I listened to him, but I didn't really believe it. I knew I shouldn't have any objection when he spoke. That he could become dangerous. I didn't contradict him. And one day, I saw. It was a painting, a reproduction in Father Audiard's almanac. There were boats in flames flying in the air. Then I believed everything. And even now, in my present state, I believe in it. When they tell me: "There is a beyond and there is either punishment or salvation", I believe that. Even though I know perfectly well that there is nothing of the sort. I am there, am I not? Therefore, I am in a very good position to talk about it.

In that beyond which is mine, there are very few things. But I believe in it. When one of my fellow companions comes and says to me: "Beware, there is salvation, but there is also punishment," I believe him. It is odd to see how many ghosts keep their faith intact. Even after death, they carry on believing. Sometimes they ponder: "All that is here is only purgatory", but in general, they don't pay attention to the fact that they are dead. They'd rather not talk about it. I say talk. But I should say: "rustle". In that cesspit of shadows, one communicates mainly through rustlings. One rustles, that's the right word. But there... Once again, I can't manage to see those moments, those flashes of childhood, without placing them in some kind of future. Future childhood. "Everything that has happened will happen again," my uncle used to say. And I believed him.

One day, my cousin took me to Ghent. We were going to visit my mother. How old could she be then? Hard to tell. For me she had remained the playmate of the dark years. We used to play “the ball that goes away”.

- What’s that, the ball that goes away?

- Here is the ball, my mother said. Can you see it? It’s like a globe, you see? Come with me, then.

We went out. The beach was greyer than ever. The wind was blowing with a kind of sneering, making my cheeks tingle. My mother looked around her. Then she said:

- Throw the ball.

It was a papier-mâché ball. Now that I think about it, it was the ball Nerval had given me at the Café de Valois. The same one, just ten times bigger.

- Throw the ball.

I did. The ball went. It was pushed by the wind. Then it stopped.

- Do it again.

I did it again. The ball stopped again. How many times did we repeat the experiment! It became tiresome. Then, coming from the sea, the uncle arrived. He was coming out of the sea, in a formal suit. Wet, obviously. He came out of the sea and approached us. He observed us without uttering a word. Then he took the ball and threw it away. The ball went. We never saw it again. How many times did I repeat the experiment (without result)? I don’t know. Perhaps I dreamed it all. We often used to play the ball that went, but it never did. It stayed there.

My grandmother shaped the balls at night. They piled up. None went. Christmas arrived, and my mother used them to decorate the Christmas tree. It was ugly, but made sense. On Christmas Eve there were no presents. But there were the balls. At midnight I chose my ball. My mother gave me a knife.

- Go on, pierce it!

I burst open my poor ball. Inside was a tiny skull. I opened a second ball. A small bone. And another, and still another.

- Complete the skeleton and you will have your reward.

I tried. But once again the uncle arrived. He was just coming out of the sea, a shell in his hand. He dropped the shell and started to fling the balls through the window. The balls went one after another. None remained.

- You shouldn't have done that, my mother said. The boy won't have his reward. And it will be your fault.

The uncle sniggered.

And that was my last Christmas Eve with my mother. The day after she left before dawn. For Ghent, the big town. She didn't want me to come and live with her. To see her, I had to come to her. However, she didn't want me to come to her. She was running a kind of hotel, an inn for sailors passing through. She was not proud of it. One day my cousin took me to her place, in Ghent, into the house of her husband's aunt. I spent the night there. Early in the morning, we went to the market. Around midday, my mother arrived. She kissed me.

- You haven't grown too much, she said.

- You remember the balls? Today it's very fashionable. Everybody wants them.

Then she started talking with my cousin. About money. After an hour, she left.

- See you next time, my child, she said.

Making the most of the moment my cousin left me by myself, I ran away. A manner of speaking, for I should say "I sold my soul". I followed my mother. She rambled in the alleyways leading to the harbour. Everybody knew her. Did I mention that she was very attractive? She was.

I followed her.

- Are you following the lady? Yes? Hey, you are too young, aren't you? How old are you?

- Fifteen.

- Fifteen! Well, let's say we share the same tastes. Let the best man win.

- She is my mother.

- That's a clanger! the man said. Pardon me, I wasn't to know. I wouldn't have said anything. But now you know. I love your mother. But she loves another. You must know all that, right? She's your mother, after all.

- I haven't seen her in years. I saw her again for the first time today.

- She doesn't like you?

- Who knows?

- Yes, that's right. Nobody knows the man she has chosen. She is fickle and cruel. Sorry again, my boy. I'm tactless.

- It doesn't matter.

- Do you know where she lives?

- No.

- Do you know if she's alone?

- Again, no.

- She is not with your father?

I didn't answer.

- Sorry. I just told you, I'm tactless.

- I'm used to it.

- You're cheeky! Is it all right if I come with you? If she sees me with you, perhaps she'll accept me more easily. Unless it's worse. Who knows?

- Who knows?

- There we are. She lives here. At least that is where I saw her enter. I've been besieging her house for a few days.

- How is it going?

- It looks like she's annoyed.

- I'm not surprised.

- Really?

We were in front on my mother's house.

- What do we do now?

The day was dark. Inside, the lamps had been lit. At times we could see the shadows of the occupants.

Someone was watching us. A good-humoured man in his sixties. He approached me.

- Do you want to board at Madame Venus' place? You're not old enough!

- Really? And what is that house? It's not a brothel, is it?

- Well, it depends. In a way, it is. Boarders live here, that's for sure. And some guests sleep here at weekends too.

Two old men entered the house.

- That's it! said my companion. A retirement home.

- Almost, the old man replied. In a way. "Shelter for the afflicted", that's what we call the house.

- Dying people, then…

- Afflicted. There's a slight difference! The house of the afflicted. Or, if you prefer, the house of troubled souls. Madame Venus brings them consolation, comfort. A bit of tenderness.

- So it's not a brothel.

- No, even though three or four women of easy virtue stay too. They are also suffering, aren't they? It is not fun every day for them.

- Shall we go in? asked my companion.

- Yes, I reply. A house for the afflicted, that's exactly what I need.

- Me too.

We knocked. My mother opened the door. She looked at me coldly. But her eyes were laughing.

- You again! I must admit I'm not surprised. Come in. And you, she said, looking at the man, get the hell out of here. This place is not for men like you. And be warned, don't insist! I'm a friend of the prefect of police. I know everything about you.

- No luck, he said. Goodbye, my friend. See you soon.

- See you soon, I replied.

The house was narrow. Like Flemish houses often are. Narrow and endless.

- Come in, come in. I didn't want to invite you in, but since you insist, come in!

She led me through to the back of a dark and humid corridor. We entered a small sitting room in which a parrot was freezing to death.

- That's Monsieur Pioul, my mother said, he is sensitive to the cold, the poor thing. When the weather is warm, he is chatty like an Indian, but as soon as winter arrives, he becomes quiet, waiting for better days.

The parrot looked at me sarcastically and pronounced a word in a strange language. It sounded like a hiccup.

He likes you, my mother said. And he is not easily pleased, just like me. Yes, he is just like me.

There was a long silence. After that, she said, almost to herself:

- You are going to stay here, I guess.

There was another silence, even longer than the first.

- If you can manage.

At the end of the corridor, someone was moaning with a sharp and ringing voice.

- Well, it's going to start. You have been told already, I suppose, here live those who suffer from an incurable ill. They are not necessarily dying. Most of them are doing quite well in fact. But they have the blues. Solitude has made their blood run cold, you see. They are not really ill. They haven't lost their appetite, they have lost the will to live. So I take them in. Now don't get me wrong, no excessive religiosity here, please. Here we just ignore their blues. You understand... that's my thing. But I listen to them, oh yes, I do! And they talk, even to Monsieur Pioul when I'm not there. He likes that, especially in the cold season. Then I play the piano. I bet you didn't know that.

- That's true, I didn't.

- Yes, I play the piano. Nothing extraordinary. Good old songs from the past. I'm happy you are here, my child. I would've liked so much to have you here. But I said to myself, all that suffering, it's not for a child.

- I am not a child.

- That's true. You're no longer a child.

- And I know a bit about suffering too.

- We'll see what you father has to say about that. He's forbidden me to have you come and live with me. He doesn't like pain, you see? What he enjoys is the life of clocks. Did you know that lately he has become a clock maker? And he's good, I have to admit. He likes order. And, as is well known, when one likes order, when one likes it to that degree, one falls inevitably into disorder.

- I thought he was an apothecary.

- He used to be a chemist, a long time ago. But he got fed up with those drug addicts, as he used to say. Since the captain's death. You did know that, didn't you?

- No.

- He killed a captain in the merchant navy. A German. Well, he didn't really kill him, otherwise he would have been put in prison. No. He even resuscitated him. But the captain was no longer himself. He was not himself at all.

- Who was he, then?

- Another person. When the captain came out of his coma, he was no longer himself, that's all.

- What do you mean by that?

- No one recognised him, not even his wife. He'd become another man.

- He no longer had the same face?

- Yes and no. Anyway. Your father gave up. It put him off, you understand? You make someone come back from the beyond, and he's no longer himself… It's enough to put you off for life. I understand him. After that painful experience, he became unbearable: he was happy with everything. "Look how beautiful it is! It is so wonderful!" It was unbearable.

- He was sad.

- Perhaps, but I cannot bear that anymore. I like well-ordered suffering. You are in pain? You are in pain! Life is tough? It is! But not that. So I asked him to leave the marital home.

- Is that what it's called?

- He left. Not alone, don't worry. He's not like that. He found himself a sweet romantic English girl, a tourist, who likes flowers, sunsets, pretty piano duets... They left. He started a new family, charming I'm told. All for the best, no? But before leaving, he made me promise that I would keep you away from that suffering I'm so fond of. I kept my promise. Until today.

- Is he happy?

- He's a clockmaker. He has two daughters, your half-sisters. That's it, really. He enjoys himself best he can.

Madame the medium suddenly feels faint.

- *Let's terminate.*

- *We are terminating the séance.*

What a shame, I was beginning to love my future childhood.

- *Yes, it's for the best, let's terminate the séance.*

FOURTH VIGIL

It was not a fainting fit she was having. It was me.

While I was evoking my childhood mishaps, I successfully "invaded" her. I have to say her mouth was open. I sneaked in. I managed to make her swallow my shadow (that's what I call my current body).

That's it, I'm inside. She is feeling dizzy. She is helped down the stairs. She goes slowly (with me inside her). She coughs (and I hold on tight, I hold on extremely tight; the smallest thing would be enough to make me leave: a laugh, an eructation). Now it's better. We walk in the half-deserted street. Here we are. Rue de F., that is where I used to live, in bygone days. Just opposite Théodore de Banville, the benevolent.

She sighs.

- I know you are there.

I whisper:

- Yes, Madame, I am.

- What do you want?

- I need your eyes. You are well aware that we cannot see, not really. We can evoke, that's what we do. Images, those shadows lit from behind surround us. That's right. But see, no, we cannot. We are deprived of that feeling of "here and now" that, in the end, is essential when one sees.

- And are you pleased about it?

- Pleased? Well, Madame, more than that, much more than that. I am absolutely delighted. That here and now that grabs you by the hair (in a manner of speaking), it's wonderful!

- And what else?

- Not much. I would like to stay with you.

- For how long?

- Hard to tell. I am inside, and it's a real miracle. I will eventually have to leave. And we will need another miracle.

- Good heavens! And can it last a long time?

- Don't be afraid. Here, in the world of shadows, nothing lasts. We could call that a paradox, couldn't we? In principle, here is eternal life. Well, it isn't. Not at all. We stroll, we float, for the moment I am inside you. Let's make the most of it.

Madame the medium sighs.

- I'm starting to feel a bit peckish.

- Well, that's good, I'm also feeling peckish.

- That's the best one I've heard.

- I know, I know! But I sneaked inside you; I inhabit you, in a way. And I cannot help but being you a bit. I mean, I feel what you feel, but as an echo. My shadows welcome your body, in the singular. Your body then gets a shade heavier.

- That's true. Let's go and eat. I don't know the area well, but I noticed a restaurant earlier. There's room.

- Let's go in.

The Brasserie de Saint-Victor is almost empty. We choose a table in a discreet corner. We will be able to talk about things from the beyond without attracting ironic looks from other customers. It has to be said that in those discussions, introspection doesn't work. Madame the medium will have to talk, to say the words. I cannot guess what she is thinking. She will have to speak, to articulate, like in the theatre. To talk to me, she turns discreetly to the wall. Which in the end attracts the attention of two or three customers.

- Speak up, nice and loud, Madame. They will think you're mad, but it will be better.

- I feel awkward.

- I know, but believe me, it will be better.

She tries. But her sense of propriety takes over.

She orders a cassoulet from Toulouse and a pitcher of red wine.

We eat in silence. Ah, that cassoulet! How did I manage to do without it?

- You are not going to tell me you're capable of eating?

- Through a medium, yes, Madame. Through the intermediary of a medium.

- And when there is no medium nearby?

- Fasting. But one can always catch a medium yawning, mouth open, miles away.

- At this very moment, are you savouring?

- Yes, Madame.

- What about the wine?

- Ah, wine!

- I must admit I don't understand anything at all. What can't you do in your world?

- One can do everything, Madame. But differently.

- Through the intermediary of a medium?

- Yes.

- And you say you can find a medium who allows you to manipulate him?

- That is you saying that. He has to consent.

- And you can smell… and savour… and…?

- Also.

- Sex?

- Of a kind…

- With a male or female medium?

- I prefer ladies.

- Well, that's a surprise!

- One cannot talk about it too much, it could lead to bad interpretations. People are so easily vexed in our times.

- Our times? What times?

- Yours.

There's a silence, heavy with suspicion. We eat in silence. The waiter arrives.

- Cheese?

- No, thanks.

- Yes, Madame, please!

- Well, yes, then! she says to the waiter.

- And which cheese would you like?

- A little bit of Camembert. And is the goat cheese hard?

- Slightly.

- Some goat cheese too, please. And a little blue, it looks good.

- All right.

The waiter looks at the lady. Without any facial expression. He carries out the order. The lady eats.

- I rarely eat cheese. But now…

- You enjoy it?

- Yes.

We eat in silence.

- You look preoccupied…

- No, it's not that. I was thinking about what you just said.

- Sex?

- Yes. I cannot imagine how it would be.

- Do you want to experience it?

- Me?

Another silence. The food goes down the wrong way. We cough.

- Yes.

- Yes what?

- The thing.

- Here?

- No, not here. It would be a bit indecent, no?

- Not necessarily, no one will notice. Shall we give it a go?

- Where?

- Nowhere! Don't move. Concentrate.

- On what? On what should I concentrate?

- On me. You have seen my portrait, haven't you?

- Yes, two weeks ago.

- Did you like what you saw?

- You are rather handsome.

- That's what people said at the time.

- Oh! But what are you doing! People will notice!

Indeed, the customers are looking at us. They don't know what to think.

- Oh! Ah! But it's incredible. I can feel everything! Oh! Yes! Yes!

- Madame?

The man at the next table has come closer.

- Oh, oh! Yes!

- We need to call an ambulance.

- No, don't do that. Oh yes! I like it!

- What does she like, exactly?

The thing finishes with a grand finale, with Madame falling off her chair. Then she closes her eyes. She looks around her. She smiles.

- Eh, you, why are you looking at me like that?

- Are you feeling better? You gave us a fright, Madame.

Another customer from another table approaches.

- Does it happen often?

- I wish! No, it's the first time.

- If it happens again, call me, I'm a doctor.

And he gives her his card.

- Thank you, doctor!

The night is splendid. We walk quietly.

- Where are you taking me?

- I'm going back home.

- Very well. I feel a bit tired.

- How can one be tired after death!? That's beyond me! It's called "the eternal rest", isn't it?

- Well, that's true. However, one gets tired. Any little thing exhausts you for centuries (in a manner of speaking).

We arrive at her place.

- Are you coming up?

- Yes. I want to see where you live. By the way, are you married?

- Yes, as it happens, I am married. But my husband is not at home. Besides, he is always away. That's why I feel very grateful to you.

A little flat, meticulously tidied. Everything is in its place.

- Yes, she says. Everything is in its place. Even you, if you wish, you could find a place here.

- Me? What about your husband?

- He doesn't believe in all that. He is down-to-earth.

- I understand.

I am tempted, I must confess, but what is a spectre if not a vagabond? A ghost is nothing but wind. One can tour the world in a blink of an eye. And the idea of seeing through the eyes of one single person would be intolerable.

She reads my mind and she understands.

- A little cognac? We deserve it, don't we? I feel drained all of a sudden. All that is quite tiring. You are a heavy burden, my dear friend. But I think I could bear you for days on end. And who knows? A whole life!

- It's time for me to go. In my condition, conjugal love is something hard to conceive.

We drink in silence.

When all is said and done, silence really is the best thing in our relationship.

- Dear Madame, please be kind enough to open your pretty mouth.

- You're leaving already?

- Yes, I have to.

- I see. Men, even in the beyond, don't change that much.

- I have to proceed with my wandering life.

- But why "I have to"?

- Would you rather I stay?

- I don't know. Yes, perhaps. I quite enjoyed your reminiscence of the childhood years.

She can say the right word. Childhood. My future childhood.

- Why do you always say "future"?

- Because my childhood never really happened. Not like that.

- Did you lie?

- No. But the reminiscence, the simple bringing back of memories can only project my childhood into the future. Do you know that in Paris in former times, I was walking one day, not far from here, with an old painter. His name won't say anything to you: Théodore Rousseau. I was in one of my bad days. Suddenly I said: "Anyway, the only thing we know is that we are born, we live and we die." He looked at me with his child's eyes and replied: "Yes, perhaps, but not necessarily in that order." At the time I didn't understand. Now I am beginning to grasp it.

- I like your spiritual side, said the lady.

- And I like your Parisian side.

- Me, Parisian? Not at all, I'm from Normandy.

My future childhood. It's coming already, I can see myself opposite my mother on the day of the auction.

The orphanage, as the people in the area used to call my mother's hotel, was opened to all and sundry every fortnight. Each boarder used to take out the objects from his cabinet of curiosities. Each had what my mother called "his own well". A casket, a box, a barrel. By definition, that well was inexhaustible. In the night, when the suffering souls were asleep, the kind soul of Ghent, I mean my mother, filled in the wells. So much so that each afflicted soul always had something to sell.

Once, there was a "saturation of desert roses". That was the only thing. A sailor, an old acquaintance of my mother, had landed. He had a whole load of them. Of all colours. The auction was a total disaster. A fiasco, as one says in Paris. In the evening, my mother couldn't sleep. She played on the piano an air, sticky like honey. Even Monsieur Pioul had fallen asleep. Suddenly my mother woke up. And she woke everybody up.

- I have it! We need to create a new profession! That's it! Divination via desert roses! That's it, it will supplement our income.

No sooner said than done. We established the rules for divination (I say us, but my mother made it all up). The customer had to bring a flower, any would do, in paper or satin, even a real one. Then it had to be compared to the still flower, the desert rose. The customer had to choose one, with his eyes closed. After, one just let the imagination take over. But the mediators, our suffering souls, "suffered", rightly. They saw everything in black, they were pessimistic. Therefore the future things they announced were terrible, in the best cases. That made all our customers run away. There were no more mentions of the orphanage, from then on our hotel was called "the cursed house". Reputations are as quickly made as they are damaged. My mother found something else, and business thrived again.

It's well known that time flies away. My sixteenth birthday arrived.

- It's time for you to pay a visit to your father. You must still have a little bit of childhood in you when you meet up. You're leaving tonight. Your baggage is ready. Everything is ready.

- Everything is ready except me.

- Really? I see you, child, I see you and I know that you are bored here. You're not suffering. It will come, but for the time being, you are bursting with health.

No sooner said than done. I left.

My father lived in a little village not far from London. I don't remember the name of that village, but I remember well the name of the property.

"The Double Path" was its name. My father was living in a mansion. It was accessible by two paths that seemed to go in separate directions but led to the same door. I hadn't taken the precaution of warning him of my visit and I arrived unexpectedly, one autumn evening. A fine drizzle was falling on the flight of steps. Everywhere there were falling leaves, a golden carpet in the light of the setting sun. I knocked and Miss Auberdine opened the door. She looked at me from top to toe, and smiled.

- We were expecting you tomorrow. But since you're here... I'm Miss Auberdine, the governess. Your father is away on an excursion. But he shouldn't be too long. Come in, the misses are having their piano lesson. They are very proper, like everything here, of course.

She left me alone in a small sitting room. I could hear someone playing the piano. It was raining cats and dogs. I came close to the stained window that gave onto the garden. A demented wind rocked the trees. I had the impression they turned on themselves, like dervishes. I heard a snigger behind my shoulder. I jumped, turned round. Nobody. On the chimney were two big portraits of my father. Why two? One, severe, looked into the distance. The other looked straight into my eyes, following me. Whether I was standing near or afar, on the right or the left, it pierced me with its extravagant eyes. I had seen that already once in Ostend. It was the avenging angel. One could accept that. But my own father...!

Soon something very strange happened: it stopped following me. Now, like its counterpart, it too had a vacant look lost in the distance. All right, I was only a child, but it was glaring: something very peculiar had happened, coming within the realm of the beyond. I already had a strong leaning towards the unfathomable, that's true. As soon as a drearily banal explanation was put forward to account for an extraordinary phenomenon, I used to feel deeply aggrieved. In my eyes, the unfathomable alone was worth my attention.

I must have fallen asleep.

A laugh woke me up with a jump. My sisters were there, facing me. One was standing under one of my father's portraits, the other had chosen her side, as one says, near the window, south with regard to me, keeping her distance, a few metres.

- Hello, I said.

They laughed heartily.

- He's so cute! one of them said. He looks much better than on the portrait we received. My name is Felicity, but you know that very well, don't you?

- He is not really cute, he's rather disappointing, that's what's good. I don't care for handsomeness. It would be too easy. It would be like a rainy day without wind. One always needs something that upsets, that doesn't go as the fur lies.

- How do you find our French? According to what we're told, we speak a very peculiar French. One that gives you goose bumps.

- No, one that makes you cry.

- No, the French of a bigot. Do you find it that thin?

- Come on, tell us. And be sincere. Because we've seen all sorts.

I didn't know quite what to say.

- I am not in a position to judge your French. I myself speak it very badly.

- He is so cute! He would rather be dead than upset us.

They were making fun of me, but with an ice-cold sweetness that brought me close to panic.

Felicity came closer and whispered in my ear:

- My sister's name is Nausicaa, but she cannot bring herself to say it.

- Why? It is a very prestigious name.

- She thinks it lends itself to incredible puns.

- I cannot see how.

- The Lord has ways and especially roundabout ways to disorientate Ariadne herself. Besides, she would have liked to be called Ariadne.

- Yes, Nausicaa said. I am far away, but I can hear you. And I don't care. And while we are at it, what do you think of our father's double portrait? Amusing, isn't it? I bet he was observing you earlier.

- Yes, indeed. Is it an optical illusion?

- An illusion! And optical, to top it all... There is nothing optical about it. It was simply him. Him, in person. He was observing you.

- Yes, he is like that, Felicity said.

I came closer to the painting. My father's face looked vacant.

- But earlier, he was looking at me.

- Of course, he was looking at you! Nausicaa said. He wants to know what kind of bird you are.

- He always says that. "What about that one! We'll see what kind of bird is going to pay us a visit."

- At the moment, he is no longer here. He's absented himself.

- But, he will expect me tomorrow, won't he?

- Not at all! Yesterday we waited for you all afternoon, didn't we, Nausicaa?

- Yes, and the weather was nice, the sun bright. Wasn't it bright?

- Much more than that, Felicity said, much more than that! Yesterday, the day was delightful. A real felicity!

- Do you know what we call Felicity at home? Calamity. It is her borrowed name. Her lucky charm, her war name.

- Stop it, or I shall pronounce your borrowed name!

- Yes, you're capable of it, seeing your love for the unnameable!

- Ah, Nausicaa! Sometimes I wonder if you really are my sister!

They sat on the floor as if they had just finished a race.

- What about your mother? I said.

There was a silence. A very long silence.

Miss Auberdine came in with three cups of tea and cakes. The sight of them put my sisters in a very good mood.

- Miss Auberdine is really adorable. A shame she has that habit of mixing everything, Felicity said. She is the one who inflicted me with that horrible name, Calamity. And, on top of that, she did it with the best of intentions. She made a mistake! That's the limit, don't you think?

- Earlier, she said to me I was expected tomorrow.

- You see! She's like that.

- And it's a shame my mother doesn't like her.

- A taboo subject in the house, Nausicaa said.

- Besides, there are only taboo subjects in this house.

- Yes, it's sad, don't you think? A house in which there are only taboos. It would be a great subject for a novel. "The house of taboos".

- Because we're warning you: we write novels. One novel a month.

- You exaggerate! Sometimes one a week.

- Yes, it depends on my father. He is, how can I say, not very fond of our novels. It seems to irritate him. And on top of that, he cannot bear others to read them.

- He finds it "not very proper".

- Well, it depends!

- Yes, for I have to tell you, our father is forever changing. Sometimes he is your father, sometimes he is mine. One just needs to be aware of that.

- Yes, we had to get used to it. Felicity has a father, and I, another.

- What about me? I said.

- Well, it's quite simple! You have two fathers.

- Nausicaa, you shouldn't confuse our brother with those ideas, he has just arrived. He comes from Belgium. That's the name of your young country, isn't it?

I am absolutely certain we had that conversation, during which they said "Belgium". But Belgium didn't exist yet. Does something exist that would be the reverse of anamnesis?

- I come from Ghent.

- Ghent, it's good to come from a place with that name. "Ghent", it's short, elegant, it tickles.

- She is talking nonsense, that Calamity.

We spent the evening chatting, nattering about this and that, or too much. We laughed, laughed so much! But there were also silences. And the silences sniggered! The silences of that house were nasty.

- Can I read your novels?

- No, that's out of the question, my father will go mad. I mean, my father… or yours, I don't know. In reality I don't know the first thing about your father!

- Taboo subject.

New wave of panic.

- And what is the subject of your novels?

- Well, says Nausicaa, it tells stories more or less taboo.

- I have an idea, Nausicaa. We cannot read our novels to our brother, but we could act them out, couldn't we? Our father gave us a paper theatre. A doll theatre, in a way. Come, we will ask Miss Auberdine to set it up in the morning room. She does that very well, with much care. She is adorable, I shall never tire of saying that.

- Even if it's a taboo subject. One more.

We settled in the morning room. The theatre was ready. A very small theatre from Denmark.

- The story is called "Cinderella seeks her cinders. A wild drama".

The curtain rose. The backdrop represented a room in a country house. Through the window, a menacing forest could be seen.

- It is Cinderella's house. She is called that because she feeds on cinder cakes. She loves them.

- No, Felicity, you are forgetting the main thing! Those are not ordinary cinders, they are her mother's ashes. Well, that's how it is: Cinderella has two sisters, one is called Triple-Eye, because she has three eyes, the other One-Eye, because she has only one.

- I am Triple-Eye. "I don't understand why attractive women only have two eyes. I have three and I'm very happy about it. I think I'm beautiful."

- "And I don't understand (Felicity makes a rough voice) why beautiful women don't have just one eye. Two eyes is common; three eyes is special; one eye is beautiful."

- Cinderella had two eyes. And she thought she was ugly, for she was modest and good-natured. We forgot to say they were living all alone in the little house here. For their mother had died, and their father, after several fiascos, had finally become a famous werewolf.

- Tell the truth, Nausicaa! The three sisters had killed their mother. You always seem to get it wrong. But it's so blindingly obvious!

- To three eyes!

Then the backdrop changes. We were in the middle of the forest.

- Here they come, the two sisters with abnormal eyes. They are walking in the forest.

- And here come two mountain hunters! They are handsome.

- "Hello, hunters!"

- "Hello, gorgeous ladies!" They haven't noticed yet that one is missing an eye and the other has one too many.

- "Come to our place," says Triple-Eye.

- "Yes, come, come, said One-Eye, we're going to cook you a delicious stew." The hunters hadn't had any luck that day. They were returning home empty-handed, and they were hungry, like everyone else.

- "We'll be there at the agreed hour," one of them said.

- When they were gone, Triple-Eye said to her sister: "Have you gone mad? With what are you going to make that stew we promised them?"

- "Well, it's easy! We'll kill our mother and make a stew with her."

- "Good idea! Triple-Eye said. It's going to be delicious!" As easily said as done! They killed their mother. They skinned her and cooked a delicious stew.

- Stop!

- Oh, Daddy's arrived. I knew it, Nausicaa said.

- Good evening, Daddy!

My father seemed a difficult character. He was returning from hunting, with three turtle doves.

He stared at me.

- Come closer, so I can take a good look at you. It is you, after all. You have grown. Come here, don't be shy.

- He is very shy, Felicity said, he didn't even kiss us. And we are his sisters, or am I mistaken?

- Keep quiet! my father said. I am the one talking here. And what exactly are you doing here? Go to bed. I shall punish you later.

- Daddy's had a drink! Let's go to bed, Nausicaa said.

Only once did he allow himself a smile. Once.

- Well, he said. You've seen your sisters, you know what to expect now. They are mad. Like their mother.

- What about you?

- Me?

He looked at me for a while. Then he walked around me.

- Me? Are you asking me if I'm mad? Yes and no. It depends what you call me. There is me and me.

- Yes, I know that. Your daughters explained that to me.

- My daughters? Not your mother?

- She hasn't been very forthcoming. You changed profession. In the past you used to be a pharmacist. You prepared a drug that made your head spin.

- Yes, you could say that. A fair summing up, I guess. But wrong. Not entirely wrong though. When I was your age, I met a doctor in Paris. An extraordinary man. He used me, I have to admit. He made me taste things. He changed me, that's it. That's all.

- And now you are another.

- Sometimes. It doesn't last long.

There was a long silence. We could hear the voices of an imaginary choir. I say it like that, but I clearly and distinctly heard the voices coming from afar. Behind the rain one could hear singing, screaming, sniggering. It was horrible.

- Don't pay attention to what the parish whispers. I call "parish" that kind of choir behind that forger rain. I call "forger rain" that local speciality, that rain which likes to hide the secrets it fabricates so much. I call "fabricate the secret" that insidious malice that imposes the borrowed malicious gossip. I call "borrowed malicious gossip"... and so on.

I switched off. I had grasped the main thing. My father's wife had died a not very natural death.

My father stared at me. The rain was beating down. And the malicious gossips coming and going. And one could hear singing. Hymns sung to the glory of the crime.

- Dead and truly dead, the voices said.

- Hung... Truly hung.

- However, she cries out!

It took me quite a while to realise that those voices were not supernatural at all. There were my sisters. They were singing, they were crying out.

Suddenly my father's smile fell on me. Like a tombstone. His smile was violent. At the same time impertinent and sanctifying. One could call it a cursed blessing.

- What do you want to do with your life?

- Nothing. I am here. I mean, here, full stop.

- Do you intend to stay? If you do, we need to take urgent measures. I detest improvising.

- I understand. So let's say... two weeks?

- Very well.

- Or perhaps, three? I can also leave straight away.

- Very well.

The smile didn't change.

That smile was addictive. One wanted more of it. More and more. People sometimes say that in Antwerp one meets Jewish jewellers with that type of smile in the harbour district. The "caustic" smile. They also are said to be able to estimate the price of a diamond with just one smile.

My father smiled like that. He was assessing the interlocutor.

I liked my father.

- Go to bed. Tomorrow it's going to be fine weather.

I was given a very cold room. I fell asleep almost immediately. My sleep was heavy and navigating.

We were in a boat. In the distance, an island appeared. An island covered in sweet wrappings. It shone like a wonderful present. From the island, women's cries and pleas could be heard. Threats too.

I woke up.

The cries and shouts were real. They were my sisters.

- No, Daddy, I beg you, not that! Don't do that!

- Daddy! We won't do it ever again!

- Daddy! No! Nooooo!

The door opened. My father came in. He sat opposite me. My sisters joined him.

- Did they wake you up? I'm not surprised.

- No, Daddy, no, or we'll tell all to the police!

- They are crazy. They are dying to be punished. But I cannot do it. I adore them. They are adorable. Like their mother. You must excuse me for this whole racket.

- She is dead, isn't she? How did she die? Murdered? By whom?

- What are you talking about? Oh, yes, her... Yes, who else, always her. Dead? Not as far as I know. She left, that's right. She wanted to start all over again. Not far from here. In London.

- Yes, Daddy! You must punish me! I deserve it! I've deserved it a thousand times.

- Not as much as me!

My father smiled. That smile, again.

- What do you think? In my opinion, they tasted my drug. All that is not normal. Unless it is hereditary. These days they talk about that, discreetly. Well, it's getting late. Even for me. Good night.

My sisters were quiet now.

I fell asleep. What an odd father, I thought, what an odd man. What about his wife? And my sisters? And the governess? Taboo?

The word "taboo" made me fall into a *cum figuris* sleep, as the priest in Ostend used to say.

FIFTH VIGIL

- Is everyone here?

- Apologies from Marmande, who won't be. Something cropped up.

- Furat is not here.

- Let's wait ten minutes. Why not take this opportunity to hear what everyone has to say?

Silence.

- Personally I find it all very exciting, Madame Friuli says. But I still believe in cryptesthesy.

- Yes, I see: the sublime cheating.

- But it's obvious! Those confessions are riddled with all sorts of contemporary elements.

- Explain yourself!

- That story of the father, without going any further. It's Dr Jekyll and Mr Hyde, right?

- When does he talk about that?

- In the last séance, of course!

Rubard takes up the notes of the last séances.

- I can't find the story of the father.

- But you know that story! Dr Jekyll. The drug!

- Yes, I remember very well. Except that I cannot find it.

- Everyone remembers the story of the father? Who hasn't heard it?

- Me, Bouvard says. The father? It doesn't ring any bell.

- Let's go back to it then. Anyway, there is something strange in all that.

- Yes, very strange. Let's recapitulate. We all took note of the adventures of our deceased friend at his father's home, yes?

- Yes!

- Yes, yes!

- Is it the same story?

- How should we know? I have a vague memory of it, but I couldn't reproduce it word for word in front of you. I thought we had a written document.

- No written document.

- What about you, Madame the medium, do you remember that story of the father, or do you have, like us, a vague memory of it?

- I remember everything.

- Really? And how's that?

- He recounted it to me.

- He recounted it to you?! Where on earth?

- Do you remember the last séance?

- Yes, you had a fainting fit.

- Precisely. And I left. Well, he left with me.

- With you? What do you mean by that?

- He took possession of my body, and he left with me. Then he spoke to me.

- And how could he speak to you, without the ouija board?

- It's a bit tricky to explain. Let's say we could communicate directly. I couldn't read his thoughts, and he couldn't read mine either.

- I guess that. So?

- Ventriloquism.

- Ventri… What?

- He spoke… I mean, I was saying what he wanted to say to me. And I replied in a loud voice, for he could not understand me if I didn't speak up.

- And what did you do?

- I won't say everything, but plenty nevertheless.

- For example?

- We had dinner together. We ate a cassoulet, quite tasty actually.

- Then?

- He recounted his childhood, well, that part we are discussing. The story of his father.

- And how is it that most of us ended up knowing that same story?

- A mystery!

- Ah no, Madame the medium, not that! If you say that, our enemies are going to claim victory! No mystery, please. Here, we think.

- Let's think.

- Let's see: did he stay long… with you?

- A few hours. He left when I fell asleep. All together he must have stayed three, four hours?

- When he left, you were in bed?

- I beg your pardon, what does it mean, all these questions? We are not in court!

- Please forgive me. But you have to admit this is all rather strange.

- Ah, as a matter of fact, he's just penetrated.

- That's how you say it? Penetrate?

- There is no other term. I can feel him inside me.

- In that case, let's start the séance. We will carry on with our chat later.

Furat bursts into the room.

- Sorry I'm late.

- You are. But since you are here, tell us what you think of the father's story.

- What father?

- The father of our subject? The late Flanders.

- Ah, that one, you mean, the pharmacist? What is going on with him? It was odd that story.

- Yes, very odd indeed, but the problem is, it never happened.

- Meaning?

- The story has not been transmitted by the ouija. It is not in the annals.

- So?

- How is it that we all know it? By what means? Telepathy, perhaps? Spontaneous knowledge?

- All right, all right! However, I have the impression I read it somehow.

- I read it too.

- I dreamt it. It was like seeing a film, except that instead of inter- titles, there was a voice whispering words in my ears, it was almost delicious.

- Was it his voice?

- My voice? Certainly not, not to you!

- It was only a dream, Madame.

- Well, let's start then.

- Is the ouija ready?

- No ouija tonight, I told you so already: the subject is inside me.

- What?

- Madame has been penetrated by the subject himself.

- What does that change?

- I want to talk to you directly, no need for writing.

- Can we start?

- Let's do it.

- Tell me. What you're telling us, did you really experience it? Or did you make it up?

- I'm making it up.

- Everything?

- Everything.

- Can I ask you what's the meaning of that act you are doing?

- It is not an act. It's a homework. It's part of our homework.

- Really, there is homework in your world?

- I go to school. I call it "the school of darkness". There we are taught how to get used to the world of shadows.

- Are there teachers, and all the rest of it?

- We learn through deduction. And through music. Here, you know it already, silence rules, but a silence made of rhythmic creaking. In that night school, we get used to the idea that everything is music, music of the darkness. Intuitively we know that the survival of our world and ourselves depends on learning that music. So we are given exercises. The most difficult is this one: to find a group of willing people who accept to listen to our daydreaming.

- So it's all false?

- No, not yet. Gradually it will all become false, I mean made up. For the time being, only my father's story is false. I invented it all. Well, that's what I thought, but my story has been refused, I have to start all over again. My father's story has been deemed unacceptable because it is too credible.

The medium speaks in a monotone voice. And behind her voice, one can hear a kind of asthmatic respiration. Mine.

In fact, I am not cheating, I am really telling my story. Except that in that story, I glide from one character to the next. Sometimes I play the good boy. Sometimes I cheat.

The medium remains silent. She starts coughing, she is out of breath.

- A glass of water, quick.

- No, let's stop for today, the medium says. *I am exhausted.*

- *All right, let's stop.*

- *Yes, but... Confusion has been sown.*

- *What confusion? We have a subject who likes to have a laugh, that's all.*

- *And who enjoys giving migraines to our medium!*

- *No, don't worry about it*, the medium says. *I'm used to it. In a way, it's the price one pays.*

- *Are you feeling all right?*

- *I am.*

- *He is inside?*

- *He is in there, yes. He's moving.*

- *Like a baby?*

- *Yes, it's a bit like being pregnant.*

They all get up and go down the stairs silently.

They cannot possibly be aware of it, but they are surrounded by a crowd of wandering souls. Souls? One should say shadows, quivering shadows. Quivering? Not all of them. Some are quite capable of staying motionless for days on end, an unusual thing and not particularly desirable, for dust (and there is never any shortage of that magnetic dust in the staircases, it has even been the object of many arguments in the meetings of the shadow-boarders), that dust encloses the soul itself. Dust "dresses" the body made of shadow and sometimes it sticks to it. And it is not easy to get rid of it.

They go down the stairs silently. The conspirators of the beyond. And on that side, the shadows fidget. Like schoolchildren during recreation.

The medium wanders off, carrying her beloved ghost with her.

They take the rue de Buci, reach the place Saint-Michel. There, she stops, as if lost.

- What now? she says (meaning, he says).

- I really don't know.

- Is there something bothering you? I feel you are uneasy.

- I am cross.

- With me?

- Who else?

- Let's go home.

- Not today, my husband is back.

- Oh, that one!

- Yes, precisely.

- And why are you angry?

- Because you played the fool.

- I played the fool?

- That school doesn't exist! It cannot exist. It doesn't mean anything.

- That's true, but, in this world, nothing is meaningful. What is foolish is to believe that all that has some kind of meaning.

- Well, you know what people are looking for. They want to receive a sign, a tiny sign, a hint of transcendence! And you come and lay it on thick with your story of school where the suffering souls learn the music of creaking. Honestly, what else now? Oh yes! The harmony of the chains one drags, the melodies of the mournful giggles! If you ask me, you read too many English novels in your lifetime. You might perturb the others, but not me! No, my dear Flanders! Not me!

- But that school, I didn't make it up. I didn't invent anything. When we went downstairs, earlier on, there was a little crowd of people in the shadows. You couldn't see them, but I caught sight of them, I brushed past them. I had to endure their jokes, and they were not particularly of the best taste.

- They were making fun?

- Yes, Madame. They were making fun of us. To be honest, they are right, we are an odd couple.

- I know.

- "So, you are bunking off with that tall girl? You prefer those from that world? You like rot?" Our story is not all that neat, you understand?

- I know that, I know only too well.

- And now, on top of it all, you are cross! Admit, it's depressing.

- I know.

- Yes, you know everything, but you do nothing!

- So, that school, does it exist?

- Of course not, I imagined it. It came into my head like that, but as you know, I just have to imagine a thing for the shadows, which are nothing but strings of will, to get agitated and conform to my spiritual representation.

- I'm no longer with you.

- I am speaking like my friend Arthur Canache. He only swore by Schopenhauer.

- Don't know him.

- Me neither, really. But he used to talk about him very well.

- So, that school, does it exist or not?

- It will exist.

- Off you go again.

- But, my lovely, I do what I can to adapt to your syntax. Here, the time, or what we understand by "time", is elastic (by saying that, I am again adapting to your syntax).

- What I think is that you're making fun of me.

- It is serious?

- Oh, you are impossible!

- I know. And I am unbelievable too!

The medium laughs. She laughs all alone, the passers-by look at her, amused.

She goes up the boulevard Saint-Michel.

- Did you imagine that life because it was imposed on you? Straight away? At school? I cannot understand what is true in all that...

- It's all true. As soon as it appears inside me. It fixes itself. It exists. And it is everyone's property.

- The living and the dead's?

- What use is it to make that distinction?

- I studied too, you know. Years ago.

- Where?

- At school, to be exact. I studied here. Here, in this wretched world, one needs to study, my dear man!

- And here it is not very different. Except that things happen in a different order. Did I say "order"?

- Yes, I understand, in your world, there is no order.

- It all happened at the same time. En bloc. Then there is that kind of start, as balls of events, en bloc, you see.

- You are dreaming!

- I say it like that, but in fact, I know nothing. Once a bloc forms, it reproduces. And suddenly there's a crowd. Each bloc contains all the things that go through our mind. It is in a way... delightful.

- You make me laugh.

- I know, up there, in your world, one doesn't laugh much. Here, we're having a ball.

- Yeah, yeah...

- By the way, where are you going?

- I'm looking for a quiet spot.

- To do what?

- Do I need to explain everything?

- Sometimes, yes.

- I want to come.

- I'm not sure it's the right time.

- I get it.

Silence. She walks, she's not happy.

- You are furious.

- Yes.

- Why? Anyway, we belong to different worlds.

- Couldn't you find a less idiotic excuse?

- Oh, I don't like to be shouted at!

- Get out!

She screams. She opens her mouth. I flee. I'm blind again. But I recall my images from the past.

I see my master Camille Flers again. We are walking slowly in the forest at Aumale. The day is breaking. It's going to be fine weather.

The frogs are croaking.

- The frogs are croaking, he says. How wonderful. Come, my boy. Close your eyes. Listen and try to see the landscape the frog is suggesting to us.

- Is it here we should settle?

- No, no, not yet. In this profession, one cannot be impatient. Are your eyes tightly closed? Well, now you need to walk, you need to walk with your eyes closed. Are you all right? Do you manage? And there is another tribe of frogs starting on your right. Do you hear them? Yes? Perfect. Let's carry on.

We carry on with our walk, eyes closed. We hear the croaking of the frogs, which becomes deafening. And suddenly, no more sound. Total silence.

- Here we are, Camille says. Open your eyes!

I look around me. I am blinded by the colours. I can barely decipher the shapes.

- Oh, a lime tree, I say. I've never seen a lime tree like that!

- Well done, my boy, you are learning fast. Well, for today you will only look. You need to see, stay where you are.

He prepares his instruments. Two paintbrushes. Or rather a brush and a paintbrush.

He starts.

He works by using both hands. At the same time.

- Yes, he says, I am like a pianist. There is the left hand for the rhythm, or, if you like, the accompaniment. And the right for the melody. And the two hands have to be tuned properly, otherwise, no work of art.

I see him painting at a phenomenal speed. The two arms move at the same time. And we can hear the music, the harmony, the counterpoint. I said "can hear": the brush has a big thick voice, a bit like a hangover. And the right hand resembles a ballerina. Sublime and impeccable.

Then I see something absurd. I see the trees around me dancing like elephants in a circus. They follow the rhythm imposed by the master turned maestro. Then I see (and when I say "I see", I mean "I see") the trees stopping and gathering behind the painter. They want to see the result of the dance. Now it's the turn of the mountains. They don't dance, obviously, but they start breathing.

It lasts the whole day. One feels the hours passing. Night falls. And Camille, indifferent, continues with his works, unperturbed. Four paintings. He places them side by side. And the paintings "communicate". It sounds like a talk at Sainte-Beuve's place.

I have the feeling I understood everything. And I understood nothing.

The day after, I took the decision to stop painting.

I didn't know it yet, but I had become "agathopède".

SIXTH VIGIL

- There are not many of us, tonight.

- It's raining. And there's a strike.

- All right. Is Madame the medium here?

- Madame the medium has a name.

- That I always forget, I'm very sorry about that. With all that's happening, my mind is not here.

- Something serious is happening?

- Well, yes.

- What, for example?

- The Three Glorious Ones.

- The what?

- Nothing, I'm not feeling myself today.

- You just said "The Three Glorious Ones".

- I said that? That's odd, I didn't want to talk about it at all.

- Well, we'd better start. We don't have the whole night, you know.

- Shall we start? The ouija board is ready? Ouija or no ouija?

- It's for you to decide, Antoine. He is inside.

- Again?

- I can't help it.

- People are going to start talking, Ethel.

- He caught me yawning.

- All right, then.

- Motion of order: I propose we do half of the séance in person... (Laughter in the sitting room.) *...in a manner of speaking, and then we go back to the ouija.*

- Let's go, Monsieur Flanders. Tell us about the agathopèdes!

- The agathopèdes? Are you pulling my leg?

- Why?

- With all that is happening, you want me to talk about agathopedy?

- What's happening?

- The barricades, the riots, the revolution, of course.

- You see? He is also thinking about The Three Glorious Ones! I am not the only one. How is that thing is in the air?

- Monsieur Flanders, tell us about The Three Glorious Ones.

- I was not there. I had to go back to Ghent. My mother was dying, at least that is what I had been told.

- So why are you talking about the barricades?

- Word reached me, that's all. I lost a few friends there, I was far away. But at this moment, The Three Glorious Ones are coming. I can hear them.

The medium stands up and walks towards the window. Her voice turns deep, solemn.

- I see people running. It's mayhem. It's the revolution. For a few months now, people have been talking about it. There were rumours going around. Well here we are. The revolution is here.

- I must confess I am a bit lost. Could there be "revenant" events like one talks about "revenant" souls? So we must conclude that a revenant (if it exists) could be attending, as such, a séance while his astral double (or phantasm) is at the same time throwing stones at the Swiss, and why not, a third part of him, as ghost to come, is walking the streets of the deserted cities of a time to come, under a bombardment from the future?

The voice of the medium grows calmer.

- I cannot answer. Sometimes there are things like bursts. An extreme situation is concentrated in a few minutes. And it manifests itself like a ghost in the singular. As I told you, there is no answer to that. Or better still, it means nothing.

- What? Is it the end?

- Of that revolution?

- If I understand, it will never end.

- How many times did you end up in the middle of riots?

- It's the fourth time. If that way of seeing things had any meaning. Because we could also say it is still here: it swells, it shrinks, it becomes hard, soft, how should I know? Anyway, that revolution is not my cup of tea.

This time it is the medium speaking in her sad voice.

- *I propose we use the ouija now.*

- *Me too, I would rather…*

- *All right, proceed.*

The medium opens her mouth. She yawns. At length. Her funny expression takes over the scene. It seems like she's about to throw up. The silence becomes heavy.

- *That's it, she says. I'm ready!*

- *Tell us about the agathopèdes.*

The medium's hands form words at a frightening speed. The words are solemn and ironic.

"As I believe I told you, I became agathopède from one day to the next. I had befriended a young anti-romantic dandy. He claimed to have been converted to anti-romanticism after the battle of *Hernani.* A battle in which I didn't take part. Once again, I was far away. To be honest with you, if you're looking for a witness to "bygone days", you should talk to someone else. I travelled that world without really paying attention to it. I've always practised the art of enlightened distraction. As soon as something crucial was about to befall me, I moved away with elegance and sadness. That's perhaps what attracted the benevolence of the agathopèdes. They were anti-romantic, as you know. But in such an intense, desperate way that they could only be called romantics. If not ultra-romantics, a bit like Arlincourt's "frenetics". Or like the parodics, whose leader was Jules Janin.

"But I was talking about that good Arnim Brabant Pathé. We were, if I am not mistaken, sitting at the Café de Valois. The owner was reading out loud a letter from the Orient, from Gérard de Nerval, who had started writing it in a godforsaken place in Ethiopia, but had posted it in Istanbul. The reading of Gérard's letters had become a kind of ritual. The owner had read, I don't know, seven, eight? Enough for the use of the word "ceremony" to be justified.

"But dear friends of the Café de Valois, do not, under any circumstances, believe the rumour according to which the Queen of Sheba had a son with King Solomon. That son came very late. When she gave birth to him, King Solomon was already history. The Queen must have been more than seventy years old. And that son had been born twice in a row, by "supernatural" means. There were thus "successive twins", one being the older by two years. They hated each other with subtlety and nonchalance. I mean they loved each other with an indirect love. They loved each other "in" the love of their mother, the eternal Queen of Sheba."

The letter was cut short brutally.

- That should be rewritten in a more convincing way. As such, it sounds parodic. We should add more nonsense to it.

I was becoming acquainted with an authentic agathopède.

I had been introduced to him the previous week, during a society evening at the home of a beautiful woman from Lima, married to the Duke of Autroie. We became friends straight away. He had a voice almost like a woman's. That of a counter-tenor, in a way, although it turned into that of a baritone when he sang (which happened quite frequently). That made me suspect he was tampering with his voice. Besides, he was handsome and he knew it. At the time, he coveted the younger sister of the Duchess. A way of speaking, for it was more like the young woman from Lima who, sometimes, was literally besieging the young Arnim.

He was in the habit of talking into people's ears, which gave him the reputation of being a conspirator. Perhaps he was after that reputation.

- So, I heard you are from Ghent.

- Who told you that?

- On principle I forget my informers, it's my secret.

- I see.

- No, you see nothing, my dear friend. But I do. And I really wish to become your friend. Or, if you want, I would like to share with you my anti-romantic ideas.

- You are anti-romantic to that degree? You want to create a movement?

- It's already done, Arnim said. And most of the so-called romantics are part of it. Are you interested?

- Not really.

- You see, with what you've just said, you already made a big step towards anti-romanticism. The world is anti-romantic. Romanticism has been a step, necessary to extract oneself from the academic corpse, but it is stillborn. And you know why? Because it is interested in Art with a capital A. They say and proclaim their contempt for all convention, but they bow to it. No, my friend, Romanticism is a "sheeplike" movement, that's all.

- But in that case, does it deserve that we create a movement with the purpose of destroying it? According to what you say, Romanticism is going to collapse under its own weight.

- That's true. But it is going to fall on us.

- We just have to move away in time.

- Well said.

- So why attack it? That can only give it extra vigour.

- And it needs it.

- How's that? Do you want to destroy or to resuscitate it?

- Both.

- I don't understand you.

- Because you are not agathopède yet.

It was the first time I heard that word.

- Agathopède?

- Young and healthy.

- Dandy, in a way.

- Yes, but above all, anti-dandy.

- Are there many of you?

- For the moment, I'm alone. Or rather, we are numerous. Do come this Thursday. We have our headquarters in the Café de Valois. Do come!

I went there. But there was no one else but him.

- I failed to convene them, I'm terribly sorry.

- I'm starting to suspect you of being the victim of your own mystifications.

- Perhaps. But perhaps the mystifications were already there and welcomed me when I came in. Have you read Hegel?

- I find it hard.

- Me too. You should read him, though.

- I trust you.

At that moment, from the back of the room, a young man with a pale face, dressed entirely in black and sporting a shaggy beard, suddenly appeared.

- Look! said Arnim. Here comes an anti-romantic romantic.

- Here comes an Englishman.

- Do you think so?

The young man approached our table as if we had planned to meet a long time ago.

- Here I am, he said, shaking hands with us.

He was American.

- Do we know each other? Arnim asked.

- Personally I do know you, said the English with an American accent.

We remained silent for a few minutes.

- German? Arnim insisted.

- Not entirely. My origins won't mean anything to you. I am Polish by adoption. My mother, whom I never knew was, apparently, Estonian, and my father, British of Turkish origin, which means, vaguely pirate. As for my ancestors, well! My ancestors come from all over the place. But I never paid attention to those things. To tell you the truth, I am Belgian.

- Just like me, I said.

- Just like me too, in fact, Arnim said.

A voice deep like a coalmine made itself heard.

- So you are the table of the Belgians! I was told about you. I was sent by a Croatian, a tightrope walker by profession, a philosopher by nature.

- What nature are you talking about? asked the false Englishman. Because, in nature, nothing is natural. I'm in a good position to tell you for I am myself a convinced naturalist.

- Here I am, claimed a fifth character. I am late! Oh dear God, Paris is not simple.

- Belgian? Arnim asked.

- Belgian by adoption.

- Like all true Belgians.

- Antoine Lévêque, at your service.

- Adelin Schwarzbrucke, pleased to meet you.

A piercing voice crossed the room and reached us, not without some charming pedantry.

- Five Belgians sitting at the same table! And in the middle of Paris! That calls for a drink!

- Belgian also?

- Not yet, but it will happen. At least I hope so. Belgian-ness is like good food, it makes itself wanted.

- You would like to join us, perhaps.

- I won't dare.

- Why not?

- Because, although you are Belgian, you are handsome like a sponge at the bottom of the Red Sea.

- Oh, we have a poet here!

- Not really.

We could hear him, but we had trouble seeing him. He was sitting at the back of the room, and the coming and going of customers and waiters made him almost invisible.

- Where do you come from, exactly?

- Who knows? Personally I always had trouble knowing that. I am incapable of situating myself. That's where my dear Belgian-ness comes from.

We could hear him very well, he had that piercing voice whose pleasing pedantism was served with Jacobin nuances.

- Please do join us!

- I won't dare, I told you so, I won't dare. You are too cute, too agathoi.

- Too what?

- Too agathoi. And you are so young. You are pranksters. You have a brilliant destiny ahead of you. All of you are destined to an original and sub-marine future.

At that moment, it was like a wave of panic: the person talking to us didn't exist, had no physical consistency. Only existed through his voice.

- No, but do stay, five is a number that attracts affection and respect. Stay what you are: agathopèdes.

We looked at each other, stupefied.

- Agathopèdes! Arnim said.

- Agathopèdes! Adelin repeated. What can that possibly mean?

- It sounds like a joke, the pirate said. (What was he called by the way? He always failed to give us his name. When he revealed he was called Robert Walker, a few months later, he did it as a confession, as if he capitulated.)

- Precisely! Arnim said. That's precisely what it was, a joke. And from now on, around this table, it will only be a matter of jokes. We have to make jokes, pranks.

- That's it, Adelin said. We have to reach "the transcendental prank".

- But how curious is that! You all seem surprised to learn you are called "agathopèdes", even though I was convened here, to a meeting of agathopèdes. Specifically here!

A long silence settled among us, like a sixth guest.

The champagne arrived. Who had ordered it?

- Monsieur Vantard, the Belgian consul in Toulon, sends his greetings. He had to leave. A train to catch.

Well, now that I think about it, it is possible that things were simpler, for we had seen Monsieur the consul. And the word "agathopède" already was on all lips before we even realised.

- I had an idea, Adelin said. Before all else, it is essential to do nothing.

- Nothing? But that's already done.

- But it is important that at the same time, everybody sees us working. We will need an office. We will compose communiqués. Anonymous letters. But always staying within the bounds of legality.

- In that case, we will have to go to the Bouchon aux Crampes.

- At Jojo's? Arnim exclaimed. Well, we'll have to organise a few duels.

- Yes, that's it, we're going to fight! I love that! Antoine said.

The first duel took place the same evening.

It has to be said that at the Bouchon aux Crampes, people didn't go to have a nice meal, but to fight. Wildly. Duels were very popular at the time. On the ground floor of the premises, there was a waiting room. Messieurs the duellists could rest there, when the swords were being used. They came and went as in a lawyer's office. There was a lot of blood too. An infirmary adjoined the waiting room. Two doctors were working non-stop. Sometimes, they even had to carry out amputations. But those were extreme cases. In that eventuality, a wrapped-up present, in which the cut member would be offered to the poor dispossessed, had to be carefully prepared. "Period humour."

Several days in a row we went there at supper-time. We had fun provoking other customers, until we had to fight several times. Our table became famous. Even the compulsive duellists thought we were overdoing it a bit.

Sometimes, all the customers of the big hall, where we were in the habit of sitting, turned away from us in an ostentatious manner as soon as we arrived. I have to say we had decided to always arrive at the same time, all together. It smelled too much of some kind of plot. Let's not forget that at the time, people used to plot with a heartening tenacity. It had become more than a fashion, a ritual with its liturgies, its passwords, its rites of passage. By mutual agreement we had decided to start the duels just after the cheese.

- *It is past midnight. I propose to terminate the séance.*

- *No objection? No objection. See you all next week.*

The medium speaks up.

- *Someone has an objection. The spirit doesn't want to stop.*

- *That's news. Why?*

- *He doesn't answer, but he is opposed.*

- *All right then. Let's carry on with the conversation.*

- *No more than half an hour though. My wife will be worried.*

- *I have work to do.*

- *We all have wives.*

- *And husbands, which is worse.*

- *Well, let's go on.*

The medium takes up the ouija board again.

- One evening, the man next to us at table, taking for pretext that we had offended Pythagoras, slapped Arnim across the face. A duel was unavoidable. As soon said as done. Dinner was suspended between the salad and the cheese.

Arnim was an accomplished gymnast. To draw blood took him three minutes.

We carried on with our meal. But someone else came over as we were having liqueurs. He had heard someone "sniggering" at our table when, at the other side of the room, the ten years of the "battle of *Hernani*" was been toasted.

Adelin picked up the challenge. But the "offended" wanted to fight us all.

He ruined the evening. Lost all the duels with three wounds in the right arm, two in the left, one in the chest and two on the left thigh.

- He lost, Arnim exclaimed, he lost without complaining! He deserves to be an agathopède!

- Precisely, said the unfortunate duellist, I wanted to apply.

- You are automatically accepted! Go to the infirmary to be treated. We will wait for you here. With champagne and a few treats.

That was it. The duels were pursued with such joy, such energy, such enthusiasm that we ended up forgetting the main purpose of our meetings. We neglected the pranks. The duels and all that goes with it, comments, technical analyses, hearsay, entirely took over our minds. We no longer talked about the *Turpitudes of the Prophet*, Rubens' *Drawing lessons*, Marc Aurele's *Memoirs*, or Pythagoras' *Treaty on numismatic*. Duels, nothing but duels.

Until the day the inevitable finally happened.

The medium speaks in a dry voice.

- The day when there was a death.

- A death?

- Who?

- Me, of course. Who else?

- This time, we terminate the séance.

SEVENTH VIGIL

Two weeks have elapsed.

- You were killed on the day of the tenth anniversary of the "battle of Hernani*". Isn't that right?*

Silence.

The medium seems distracted. She is elsewhere.

- Do we need to repeat the question?

- He refuses to talk.

- About what?

- About that.

- That what? The battle or his death during the duel?

- He wishes to talk about his childhood.

- His childhood, where?

- In Ghent, at the hotel of the suffering souls.

- Fine. But I'm a bit lost. I'm not talking for my colleagues, but as far as I'm concerned...

- No, I'm fine! A few weeks ago he refused to talk about his childhood, now he wants to go back on it. I'm in favour of that.

- Me too, but for different reasons. Because I adore the mosaic side of the whole thing.

- But surely, we are dealing with science here, not art!

- I thought we were practising the "medicine of the beyond", and medicine is an art!

- Please, no metaphysical discussions here.

- And why not? I thought it was precisely what we were doing here, metaphysics.

- We are not at Monsieur Bergson's, as far as I know!

- I thought that was exactly what we were planning to do by inviting Monsieur Bergson to our séances.

- He refused. He refused! Let's not mix everything!

- For goodness sake, show some restraint!

- No, yes, fine, but the "medicine of the beyond"...?

- Monsieur Flanders claims that the little treaty on medicine of the beyond was one of the agathopèdes' projects.

- Yes, of course, what else now! If we were to believe him, the agathopèdes invented everything!

- Fine, fine, I give in, let's hear about that childhood.

- In Ghent.

- In Ghent and beyond. I stopped at the murder of Monsieur Flanders' stepmother.

The medium consults her ouija board.

And the visitor carries on with his story.

- I see, I "foresee" for the moment the town of Ghent. I say "I see" because it is extremely painful for me to know in advance (I say that while considering your restrictive chronology, that, I must admit, comes back to me from time to time, like an icy wind, like a secret whiff, as our dear Nerval would say). Considering that special chronology, my childhood scenes shape and lose their shape, like spring clouds. And I see a very special day taking shape, there, in Ghent, a day of auction at the hotel of the suffering souls. I already mentioned the desert roses.

- Does someone have something to say?

- Yes, me. I would like some clarification concerning that kind of pointillism which, according to Monsieur Flanders, is the source of the formation of memories.

- He accepts, the medium says.

- I accept. But I am not familiar with the word pointillism.

- That's correct, we don't live in the same epoch.

- Yes, of course we live "in the same epoch" and "in the same era". I have to mention to you that this séance of what you call "spiritualism", I've already experienced it, but the other way around. At the suffering souls' place, the first time, and with the agathopèdes a few days before my death.

- How's that? The revenants...?

- It was you. Some of you. Your medium. I am sure about her. And others. But it's coming. It's already coming... the day that is happening

at this very moment is precisely that of the séance in question. And the mediator, the medium, it was precisely "the desert rose".

The day had been dull and murky like some days in Ghent can be. The fog was more yellowish than usual. All the lamps had been lit, and the ghostly silhouette of the suffering souls was one with their glistening shadow. Around five o'clock, the last customer left. The suffering souls settled around the main table, where the most beautiful desert rose was waiting for us. It looked like a magic lamp. Fascinated, we looked at the gleam coming from the inner petals. There was something happening "there". Tiny shadows, positioned in a circle. As if they were around an invisible stain, but turning, their eyes closed. They were asleep. And I saw you! And then... We heard, coming from far away, your voices like mice's, like a bird song, grating, not pleasant, terrible. At the beginning, we didn't understand what you were saying. And then, gradually, your voices became more distinct. You were saying numbers. You were reciting the hours. "Midnight, one o'clock, two o'clock, three...", and then, from time to time, a voice was saying: "Someone is knocking at the devil's door." And it started all over again. How long it lasted, I don't know.

- Well, my mother said, since those figures from beyond the sea have been imposed on us, let's pretend to be those who convened them.

- Who are you and why are you here?

- One of the figures, now I can say it was you, Madame the medium, opened her eyes. She looked at me.

- You called us.

- We? Never! my mother said.

- We are here calling a man who belongs to the kingdom of shadows.

- Who? my mother asked. There are no ghosts here!

- Monsieur Flanders, the medium insisted.

- What do you want?

- We've been summoning you for two séances already and you refuse to come to the summoning.

- What do you want?

- One of the participants wishes to know how the day of your death was.

- My death? I am fifteen and I feel quite healthy.

- Last time, you told us that you died in a duel.

- What an idea! I am tempted to ask you how was your death.

- We all died on the same day, at the same time, in a fire. We were summoning you when the lightning struck our salon.

Then the desert rose became wan. At that moment, lightning struck in front of our hotel, causing a slight panic in our neighbours.

- The loop is looped, my mother said. One should say Ghent is waving goodbye to you in a particularly brilliant way. You are still leaving tomorrow?

- Yes, mother.

- At dawn?

- At dawn.

- You won't forget your desert rose, you need to show it to your father. That desert rose is a clock, and your father, I heard, has become a master clockmaker. It will certainly interest him. He has a sense of humour and is a little fond of the unfathomable. He will be delighted with it.

I went to bed early. I took the desert rose. I placed it on my bedside table. I didn't want to forget it when I left at dawn. Now I know I couldn't have forgotten it.

Around midnight, a tremor awoke me. I looked around me. Total darkness. I was about to fall back to sleep when I saw a tiny light. It looked like a shooting star. It was coming closer. It was coming from the desert rose. Then I felt the desire to play a prank: the flower had woken me, it was my turn to awaken it.

- Spirit, are you there? I said, laughing.

Other laughs responded to mine, like a far away echo.

- Who is there?

- Edmond la Fourme, the spectre said in a nasal voice.

- Who are you?

- Someone who wishes you well.

- Where do you come from?

- From the world of darkness.

- What do you want?

- To warn you. You must destroy the desert rose.

- The rose? I cannot, it's a gift for my father the clockmaker.

- It is absolutely necessary. This fatal rose wants to annihilate you. It's going to kill you like it has already killed us.

- When did you die?

- The 3rd July 1920.

- Are you making fun of me! We are in 1825.

- Look at the rose! Go on!

I obeyed. And I saw something impossible to convey. It will suffice to say "I saw". It was no longer a desert rose, it was a whirlpool of small soap bubbles.

- There is no reason to be alarmed, I said. Just some soap bubbles.

At that moment, another tremor made me jump. It was hot. I was suffocating. I opened the window.

There was a knock at the door.

- Are you there? Everything's fine? Are you all right?

It was my mother. I was groping in the dark. I almost fell two or three times, finally I managed to open the door. But at that instant lightning struck again. It struck the desert rose, which exploded like a bomb. And a marvellous firework invaded the room. Thousands of bubbles of all dimensions flew in all directions and finally escaped through the window.

- Son, you saw nothing! You saw nothing! my mother shouted, and she dropped dead.

I lost consciousness.

I woke up early. I was lying in the middle of the room, dead cold. I heard my mother's voice. She was singing. She was preparing breakfast downstairs, in the kitchen, as if nothing had happened.

- Mother, are you all right?

- Why are you saying that? Did you sleep well?

- Yes, mother, but I think I had a nightmare.

- Normal! I slept very badly too, with that electric storm. It all broke loose, yesterday evening, the suffering souls barely slept at all, poor things!

- Mother, what exactly happened?

- Where?

- Here.

- Why are you asking me that?

- Lightning came in through the window. It struck the desert rose.

- The desert rose?

- I haven't found it yet.

- Well, I put it in your baggage, to make sure you wouldn't forget it.

That's for the first "visitation" (I've always called it that).

The second visitation happened on the same day. Barely had we started the crossing. The sea was threatening. As the sailors say. "The face of the sea was not welcoming, it was looking at us the wrong way." Up there, the clouds were dancing with a kind of litigious severity. From time to time, a pretty face emerged, as if coming from the moon. The moon, it should be said, was there, vigilant like a lantern. Once more (the third time, I think) it had taken the colour of bad encounters. It was green. A detestable green, like a soldier's whistle. It started to rain. It was an inconsolable rain, greenish too. And virulent. To sum it up, I was sad, I was feeling as miserable as a coalman's cart.

Then behind me I heard my uncle's voice.

- Be careful, beware of the paper balls!

I turned round, just in time to duck a paper ball that brushed past my head, and disappeared into the horizon. Then a second ball bounced on the deck and flew away towards the clouds... There was a third, a fourth. A real bombardment. And then finally (why do I say that?), it was predictable like the shouts of the sailors, the ball crashed onto the deck, where it burst into a thousand newspaper sheets. The wind blew away almost all the sheets, except for one. I read it. One could see a group of people dressed in an extravagant way (years later, I understood that illustration was what was later called a photograph). I recognised the apparitions that the desert rose had shown us the day before my departure. I recognised you, ladies and gentlemen, I had the time to read "the victims of lightning" before the wind took away the sheet.

The rest of the journey passed without incident.

- And then you arrived at the home of your father, your half-sisters, and the whole caboodle. But after?

- I stayed at my father's for three weeks. Three unforgettable weeks. My half-sisters played at seducing me. They were jealous of each other, I let them get on with it. It rained, it was always raining. As for my father, he had gone travelling. In Switzerland. Some kind of convention for

clockmakers and masters in automatons. He was supposed to hold a conference on the theme: "Is there a future for soft clocks?"

- I prefer a thousand times when he's at home, Nausicaa said. He is less troublesome, do you understand? Now that he knows he is far away, he is going to pester us with his stories of "close beyond" and "aquatic time". To be honest, I'm slowly beginning to be fed up with it.

- On the other hand, I am game for daring an excursion in to the secret workshop.

- The secret workshop? I said.

- It's a bit exaggerated, Felicity retorted. In fact, it is a disaffected church with a few clocks added to it...

- Let's go, Nausicaa insisted, it should be fun... You'll see, it will be like visiting our father's head. You have to deserve it, you understand?

- I'm not sure I understood it all, Felicity sighed. It is the presence of our mother that complicates things.

- She died "suddenly", as the newspapers had it.

- That happens. Even in our close entourage. Swift death, sudden death is a daily event.

- But to go to the extent of putting it in an epigraph...

- Yes, I know, she's making a spectacle of herself!

- Sometimes she appears completely naked. It gets annoying in the end, don't you think?

- Our brother is dumbfounded. And I understand him...

We were devouring a truly unreasonable quantity of toffees.

The three images of my father observed us maliciously. I hadn't even seen the third appear.

- Will he ever leave us! Nausicaa said.

There was a combination of pride and annoyance in her voice.

- Be honest, her sister said, admit you like it! After all, it can only mean one thing: our father is mad about us, isn't he? There is madness behind all that.

- He only lives for his machines.

- And his machines have one single purpose: our happiness.

- The "idea" he has of our happiness. A very particular idea of our happiness.

- And about happiness in general.

- And, as always, it can only lead us to an atrocious death.

- Stop it!

- No, nothing nor anyone could stop me! I'm telling you what I think! My father has found a very original way to push us to commit suicide: he deprives us of air. It can only lead to asphyxiation. Apnoea and all that.

- Are you serious?

- No, of course not, I'm saying that for a laugh.

- Admit that you want to annoy our brother… He is petrified.

- Poor thing. But he asked for it…

That was true, I was in a state close to panic. But it was not so much because of the conversation: the three animations of the father were following our dialogue. And he was moving his lips.

There was a long silence, but our father's lips carried on moving! They were saying… They were making threats of a disturbing sweetness. He loved us, it was blindingly obvious. But why so much zeal!

Three animated images. We could even guess what he was saying. Each image had a discourse that was its own. The first was talking finances, it was threatening. The second was talking frankness, and it was simply insulting. The third was just soothsaying natural disasters, it was prophetic.

Felicity, the most natural in the world, came closer to the first image and erased its mouth. With an eraser.

That left me dumbfounded.

- Yes, Nausicaa said, Felicity is an eraser girl (one can say that, right?).

- An "eraser girl"?

- She erases everything! That's the only thing she likes. I did tell you, didn't I, about the day she decided to erase everything. Everything! Are you shocked? No? Fine. She erased everything! Me, the governess, the house. You also. Even though at that time, you didn't exist (in a manner of speaking), you were not part of our life yet.

Nausicaa closed her eyes.

- I admit I'm a little disappointed by your lack of amazement at our efforts to make you enter our world. You don't do amazement, do you? Is that it?

I didn't know what to reply.

- You will excuse me, my darling sisters, but I didn't know I was supposed to be amazed.

- But everything we say is amazing. Isn't it? said Nausicaa.

- I thought I was supposed to pretend nothing was untoward.

- Like one listens to the rain falling down, Felicity added.

- But surely you must have understood we wanted to amaze you with our exquisite turns of phrases.

- That word again!

- What now?

- You shouldn't say "exquisite". Our brother won't understand. We want to amaze him, not to exclude him. You will have to forgive her, my friend. But we have to accept that damned habit of saying "exquisite".

My father's voice mixed with the delirious words of my sisters. It whispered recommendations full of common sense: "Don't forget to close the windows", "No swearing", "Do like the clocks", "Cast your net wide", "With time, no volunteering."

Then other voices mixed with my father's and with the giggles of my sisters.

- We should terminate the séance.

- The medium is exhausted.

Nausicaa remained motionless, as if suspended in the air.

- What is that?

- Our father is not alone, there are women with him.

- How's that, women? He is not alone?

- I can even hear another man's voice. Right now he's saying: "Close the windows, or the future will suffocate you!"

- Well, really!

Then, with great amazement:

- Oh no!

- Enormous. Enormous...

Silence.

If I understand the situation, gentlemen, regular members of the spiritual society of the Île-de-France cannot digest a practical joke, all in all rather common with us agathopèdes. It's been a while that we belong to the world of darkness. Alas, practical jokes never stopped.

Now, those nice people bustle around a desert rose.

- Teleportation! That was not planned in our programme.

- Let's terminate the séance.

Three members of the society stay in the salon. They examine the desert rose with a magnifying glass.

- Teleportation?

- Yes. Teleportation!

- What can we do with that?

- It had been decided that the purpose, the sole purpose of our proceedings, was spiritualism.

- Spiritualism! Nothing but spiritualism!

- On no account was it about teleportation. Even less about teleportation of objects from the other world.

- Unless...

- Yes, that's it. Unless...

- Parallel worlds? Is that what you are thinking about?

Hearing that, I am taken aback. What are they talking about, exactly? I am beginning to think that those nice people are agathopèdes without knowing it. One shouldn't forget that I hear their voices as if they came from behind a curtain, they all sound similar. On top of that, I am blind in that world.

- Thinking about, that's the word.

- Even in that case, the problem remains.

- Exactly, we had said and said it again, the purpose of our venture was the creation, the elaboration of a secular theory of dialogue with the dead. One should never forget that. Well, from that point of view, we couldn't have chosen a more atypical subject.

- That's true, but if we want the theory to be, let's say, scientific, we have to accept there is no atypical subject.

A long silence ensued.

- But what is it all about, if I may ask? Cryptesthesy, isn't it?

- It's about the implicit memory that enables a medium to reinvent a deceased person. To resuscitate him "larger than life", as one says.

- In this case, cryptesthesy doesn't explain everything.

- We have to see how to integrate the new facts.

- Ah! All that dispirits me.

Silence again.

Someone pours cognac into the glasses... I know it's cognac.

Nothing else. In the end, I feel irritated. Those people annoy me. Do they realise what they are doing? They are making an innocent suffer. I agree, I am only the shadow of my former self. The shadow of a shadow even. That's the truth! Darkness is worn like a hat, like an umbrella. How do you explain the distress of a man who wanders under the rain for all eternity? Besides, there is nothing worse than "inner" rain. I've already said it somewhere: here all is drizzle, mist, it rains and rains. And we walk, head leaning to the left (never to the right). Between the rain and us, the boundary is indiscernible. We are the rain. Someone said it: each drop that falls on us is like a little weakness that tickles us. We are the root, the tree is the rain. That is the reason it rains in this salon where the secular spiritualists sip their cognac. What humiliation!

I leave the place quietly. But someone exclaims:

- *He is leaving!*

- *How can you possibly know? I've heard nothing.*

- *Cryptesthesy, I guess.*

I go down the stairs. It drizzles dreadfully. A little while later, I hide beneath my staircase. It's raining cats and dogs in there. I give up. And remain on the same spot.

Soap, my dear tramp, arrives. He's in an excellent mood. In his world, the weather is nice. Today is full moon.

He takes out a bottle of poor wine, and guzzles a good half of it.

Then he sighs and lies down opposite me. He looks at me, and I see myself through his eyes. Thanks to him the rain stops.

Here's the world as he likes it to be seen: chaotic, cacophonic, cataleptic. Suddenly the figure of Arrekx comes back to my mind.

I see him again, sombre, aggressive. He comes up to me with his horselike manners and his bad boy look. As usual, he shows off, exhibits his "pirate" black nails. He slaps me across the face with a chilly smile, darker still than his nails. Arrekx. The old fox.

- Why is it that when I see you, I don't see my eye looking at you? he asks.

And as usual, I don't reply. Noticing he hasn't managed to surprise me, he changes subject.

- It's raining, but I don't believe in it.

Stunned, I look around me.

- It's not raining… I think…

He gives a laugh heavy with menace.

- You make fun of everybody, but it will end up badly.

- I know.

- No, you don't know, you poor idiot!

Here's Arrekx as we used to see him every evening at the cellar of the riverain. Arrekx the "obscure". Arrekx or the "apocalypse"!

- You are going to die soon, the sooner the better. Let's meet up tomorrow, at eleven, Café de Valois. We will all be there.

- That's settled.

He disappears… It's raining again. My heavenly tramp is no longer there. In his place, he left rain. A rain both ferocious and calm…

Suddenly Soap is back! Where did he come from?

Yes, it's me, that kind of thing, that fog. It's me, that ferocious rain.

- What's the matter… Are you crying?

- The question surprises me. In our world, it's well known, we don't cry: the rain is one thing, but tears… Certainly not that.

- All right, all right, don't feel dejected.

I look around me (but with what eyes?)

- Are you there? My beloved tramp, are you there?

I sense something like a hollow whisper.

- I live in pure duration.

- Really? What about me, then?

- You? You glide, well, I guess.

- Each time we start having transpersonal exchanges (that's how those gentlemen spiritualists call the chats from beyond the grave), each time we try to agree on any point whatsoever (like it's raining or not, for example), we strike a jarring note loaded with insults and malicious grief. Madness is not far away.

- Madness is never far away, my beloved tramp retorts.

How could he possibly have ended up here with his culture, his finesse, his sharp mind, always aroused?

- I am not normal.

That's odd, I'm thinking and he answers. And at each retort, he seems to change worlds.

- I live in pure duration…

He is not normal, we all agree, but what normality are we talking about here?

- Normality is to have an immediate answer whenever one wishes.
- Well, that makes sense!

He is not normal, that's clear, but, in that case, why does he look so proper? Normality itself! Except for that manner, let's say, jerky, to enter duration and leave it with a pleasant ease that doesn't quite succeed in hiding its sordid aspect. Indeed, to say things clearly, it is well and truly an escape. He is the typical escapee. What he calls "duration" is nothing but the endless tunnel of what is done and undone.

There, sitting in the alcove under the stairs, he nonchalantly observes spectres going about their daily business...

Obviously he thinks he is the only one to see them.

- It is raining a lot in your world, he says, just like that.

He is therefore capable of seeing "rain". He sees us.

He takes a yellowish notebook from his bottomless coat and starts transcribing what I just thought. But can we call "thought" that egocentric discourse in that fluvial duration of the beyond?

He transcribes.

Everything about him is ceremony. Solemnity, pomp, the grandiose are part of his daily life (well, it depends on what we call "daily" life). Each moment. Each segment of a moment (it's him who says that).

- Before I forget: I was "called". Rather I should say "summoned".
- Who? Where?
- I don't exactly know. It doesn't happen here, I mean, in these times. In that place there is a fairground. With many machines, automatons with illumination all around them. Under the snow. I understood it was not far from the South Pole.
- And what were you doing?
- Well, I was dead. I was a revenant or something like that.
- How do you know?
- They were seated around a table.
- With a ouija board? Still?
- Still.
- And I bet they were still saying: "Is there anybody there?"
- Still.

- But it's too silly for words! Nothing changes!

- No.

- So if I understand correctly, there you play the same role as me here?

- You call that a role? Well, why not? Yes, I am a revenant, there! That's how I make my sleep profitable.

- Well, that's something!

- As you say. I am like everybody else.

- Do you think so? Do you really think so? Do you think we all are revenants?

- Ah, my friend, what we call "soul" is just a key. Just a master key. And I'm telling you they want to summon you.

- Who, me?

- Yes, you, yourself. Well, it depends what you call "self".

- A second-degree revenant?

- Is that how they call it? I don't know. What they wish for, I think, is a spirit with some experience. You know, it's not obvious but it is a profession to be a spirit. First you have to be careful not to blabber. We are not summoned to talk nonsense. I say it like that, but I've known more than one who've got it into their heads (it depends what you call "head") to preach a return to religion. And one knows perfectly well that there is nothing, absolutely nothing, after death!

- What about us, then? Are we nothing?

- Less than nothing!

- Well, well, all right then! I understand, you pretend this life that we live is worth nothing... But we are here! (Well it depends what you call "here".)

- Are you interested?

- In what?

- The journey.

- Why not?

- Because it needs to be prepared, do you understand?

- I do.

- So, you do agree?

- Yes.

- You need to know: if you are quite successful, you will be summoned up again. I, without going any further (it depends what you call "further"), I, for example, am disturbed all the time, sometimes even during the day. And I am alive. Do we still have an agreement?

- Still, yes. Generally they call around what time, I mean in your world?

- At the time of the octopus. Four in the morning. Including the time difference, for they are calling you from the Antarctic territory.

- Is that far away?

- Very far. Well, it depends what you call "far away".

- Not further away than the distance that separates you and me?

- If you like! Is it still a yes?

- Still.

- You asked for it.

- And how do you feel about being alive here, and a ghost there?

- I am lucky. If you like, we all are "here and there". And even elsewhere. But we don't know it, that's all. You, for example, are in an endless number of places, doing and saying the same stupidities. Fortunately you are not aware of it. So you bear it, you get used to it, you accept it. But I'm warning you! If you were to start travelling, to accept invitations, summonings here and there, you would be likely to end up in quite a mess. Oh yes, my poor friend. Do we still have an agreement?

- Still.

- Then, let's be patient!

- But when you say "to be successful", what are you talking about, exactly?

- The number of summonings. Assiduity.

- And… it pays well?

- If you like. They can flatter you. They have a way…

- It's already better than my cryptesthesists…

- *Cript* what?

- Nothing, the people from the third floor… They just annoy me. Flatter? I know nothing about that. On top of that, they refuse to believe in my existence. Mind you, me neither.

- Well. But you are game, right?

- Yes… Well… I guess so. Why not? Here we're bored stiff.

- That's a yes! he shouted, as if addressing I don't know whom, on the floor above.

I look around me. At the beginning, I see nothing. Only white. After, it gets worse. I feel rocked by some kind of milky smoke. Behind that I make out a few pale, haggard faces. They are five, or perhaps six, without counting the one who makes me see.

- That is fantastic! a baritone voice said. We are in the presence of a revenant coming to us from afar.

- Not from far away… I perform in Paris. Here specifically.

- That's debatable… Here is not Paris. Perhaps it was Paris. A long time ago.

Behind all those faces emerges a unique smile that makes them all brothers. Yes, just like a smiling horizon line that would cross all those faces before being lost in the distance. There, right in the middle of that plain covered in snow, there is one single burst of laughter that makes me wonder.

- Yes, I say it and say it again: it is fantastic!

I cut him short.

- What are you expecting from me?

- Nothing, we are just having a laugh, says the man with the ouija.

And again, reaching us from afar, that laughter, sharp and ringing.

- On the other hand, a woman's voice says, I would very much like to know if a ghost with your experience can fall in love.

- I can only answer yes, three times yes.

- And… did it happen a long time ago?

- It is happening right now.

- Can I ask you who is the lucky one?

- Of course: it is my medium. I regularly fall in love with my mediums…

- A spiritual love, I presume?

- Not entirely.

- There is no sex involved, surely!

- Well, as it happens, yes. It is not exactly what the living call "sex", but it is quite similar…

- That is extraordinary!

- I told you so. An experienced revenant will gain attention, my heavenly tramp remarks.

- But is he also there? That is quite remarkable!

Now I can see more clearly. An almost empty room. A single window, through which one barely sees a white, blue landscape… No vegetation. In the distance, a red river. From time to time objects in flames, like boats, cross the green sky.

- It's three times fantastic, the voice of the enthusiast says.

Once more I cut him short.

- What are you expecting from me? Or should I understand that you will just enjoy my presence, nothing more?

- No, no, another mutters. We like true stories.

- Yes, yes, real-life stories, nothing but real-life stories…

- But, on the other hand, improbable too.

- Yes! Above all, improbable!

- We would like to take note of your non-existence.

- Well, of life as you imagined it.

- Or better, of a life different from the one you happened to be part of for a few decades.

- An imaginary life! For what? You don't need me for that.

- Alas, yes! We have no imagination!

- Everyone has imagination!

- Not us. It exists, obviously. It is not so far away. But it eludes us. It slips through our fingers, if I may say.

- That's why we undertook the task, the vast task of inviting the spirit of the imaginary to visit us. We had developed a programme.

- A programme financed by the ultimate regions.

- Because in reality, what is imagination? Nothing else but the development of a certain "ready wit".

- An altered ready wit…

- That would gnaw at the spirit of geometry, so as to force it to produce an object with no purpose or destiny.

- Non-existent objects that reach us, out of line with our lives…

- And that disturb us!

I don't know what to answer.

- In reality, we are looking for the "spirit of the staircase", what is known as the "wit of the staircase".

- That's why your presence is indispensable, you see. According to our friend, you live in a recess, at the bottom of the stairs. You are the "spirit of the staircase", that's right?

- Ah, I'm beginning to understand what you mean by "loss of imagination".

- What? What do you mean by that, exactly?

- I'm sure that dear gentleman from the Staircase understood us.

- What a pretty name!

- My name is Flanders. Besides, I am Flemish.

- One should never be ashamed of one's origins.

I'm starting to see more clearly. There is a big table of intimidating whiteness. In front of each participant, there is a small incandescent mirror, sparkling with numbers and letters that transcribe my barely formulated thoughts (sometimes even before they are formulated). The walls, apparently empty, are in reality decorated with tiny lights. That gives it the appearance of a starry sky. By contrast, the ceiling is invisible, hidden in the heavy darkness.

Time passes. Nobody speaks. I'm getting impatient.

- But what are you expecting from me?

The walls sparkle, panic-stricken.

- Nothing.

- Nothing and everything, let's be clear!

- We have a proposition. For us, it is very important, urgent even! Our survival depends on it, if you like...

- Our survival and our hereafter. Do you get it? Our future life as ghosts. Our eventual resurrections.

- Our transpersonal exchanges.

- What about me, in all that?

I hear a colossal laugh, but the faces remain imperturbable.

- Your friend told us that at the moment, you spent your time recounting your past life to a group of enlightened spiritualists, who, it appears, want to prove a theory according to which you don't actually exist.

- That's the limit, isn't it?

- We, on the opposite, are definitely more realistic. We wish to invite you to tell us an imaginary life, yours.

- And we will believe you, dear sir. We will believe you.

- And we really hope that this time, your inventions are going to save us!

- It is definitely more generous than to want to prove your inexistence from the true story of your life among the living.

- If indeed I follow you, what you want is for me to imagine a life in which you will believe wholeheartedly.

- Yes, yes!

- Well, well… I confess I'm quite incapable of following you. But to imagine for myself a different life than the one I was given to live, quite suits me.

- I knew it!

- I ought to start straight away, I guess.

- Oh no, no! We are not monsters, you know… You have time to think, you can have all the time you want.

- And what do I gain from all that?

- You will gain a life.

- What life?

- The one you are going to make up for our greatest delight.

- You will gain the privilege of living "for real" what you are going to imagine.

- And you, what are you gaining in the operation?

- We will have the incredible privilege to study you, to see the functioning of a living being equipped with all the tools that imagination provided humans with in the past.

- We will be able to have access to a human being who imagines! You cannot possibly know to what degree it all is indispensable to us.

I don't know what to say. Suddenly I lack imagination…

- I have difficulty imagining the absence of imagination.

- You see? Saying that, you are already showing imagination. We are incapable of doing that…

- All right then, we will "do that". You will have to take pot luck, though. I don't have a method.

- Phew! Method, that's the only thing we have got.

- All right, I'm waiting for your orders.

- Well, that's not for now. We do have your agreement. After that, we will still need to take a few purely bureaucratic steps.

- Yes, grants, and all that.

- We will contact you.

Everyone disappears.

- *Is there anybody there?* the voice says.

I had almost forgotten. I float in the warm air of the salon that is used as an office by the cryptesthesists.

The atmosphere is loaded with animal magnetism. I feel rocked by those sighs, that breathlessness. It is like tremors, like turbulences.

In the end, I am gobbled up by my very dear medium.

And I can finally see the whole scene: they are all there.

- Yesterday, we were worried for you.

- Yesterday? I don't know. Earlier on, I was elsewhere.

- Elsewhere? Doing what?

- Elsewhere where?

- Elsewhere in time. And in space. South Pole, in a future century.

- But were you summoned "without consultation", as one says?

- Yes. I was entrusted with a mission. A delicate one.

- Well then! That's the best one yet! I'm telling you, my dear Albert, that if what he says is true, your theory will be compromised.

- I don't see why. He speaks, he makes it up, he rambles. We take note, that's all. He can say whatever he wants, the fact remains that nothing, nothing he tells us is real. Our medium imagines for us. She believes, of course, everything she invents, but we are not forced to follow her in her daydreaming.

- Motion of order: we don't need to argue in front of our guest. If, and that in spite of our convictions, it is ever proven that he exists, or has existed in real life, we would have committed an act of intolerable cruelty. He suffers, dear friend!

- He doesn't exist.

- Someone is suffering.

- Motion of order: yesterday, we had decided to ask him two questions: when and in which circumstances did he die, and in which type of agathopedic actions did he take part? In the end, we asked him to describe in great detail a personal adventure, easy to verify, and which no one except himself could possibly be aware of.

- That's it. Although I persist in thinking there is a contradiction in the last proposition: "easy to verify" implies that there has been a witness.

- I totally agree, let's say: "which our medium couldn't have been aware of in other circumstances...".

- Should I understand you don't believe in my existence?

(It is me speaking, but the medium vocalizes).

- Yes, Madame, but...

- *Madame? I beg your pardon, gentlemen! I belong to the stronger sex.*

- *Although I find it hard to admit the adjective "strong" could be applied to you.* (It is her speaking, but oddly enough, she has taken on my accent.)

- *Sorry, Madame, we often use the adjective "strong" to say that the person we are talking about is a man...*

There is silence. A long silence.

- *Well, first question.*

- *You wish to know the circumstances in which I met my death?*

- *Yes. And easy to verify, I'm begging you!*

- One can say (I can say to you) that the day of my death, if I remember well, was particularly peaceful. Peaceful and even joyful: Parisian sun, pure air, pleasant temperature. Up early, I went for a walk. I took the rue de Rivoli, and walked down as far as the Tuileries. I was singing an air that had stuck in my head: "I don't believe in love." It was Jenny Colon who had made it popular, I believe. Hearing me, the pedestrians took it up too with real conviction, and often the whole street was singing it. It was delightful. One shouldn't be surprised then if, coming out of nowhere, my dear Gérard de Nerval appeared. He didn't seem surprised to hear everybody singing the song of his beloved. I found myself before him. He smiled at me with that kind of disturbing good-nature he sometimes affected, and said to me:

- Jenny just died. Actually, I'm not sure she would have liked that tribute. She didn't really like that song. She even claimed that just hearing it or evoking it during her hours of insomnia, gave her a rash.

- When did she die?

- In a week's time, poor thing.

- A week ago!? Nobody seems to know!

- In a week's time, there's a slight difference. That's why nobody knows. Nobody! It's a secret. The best kept secret in Paris... She doesn't even have a scent of it. Yesterday evening, can you imagine, we made a few allusions, some friends and I, to her decease. Extremely discreet allusions, one has to say. She was there, before us, quietly sipping on her glass of aniseed. No reaction! Can you imagine? As a joke, I even exclaimed: "Jenny is not dead. This morning, I spent three hours pacing up and down the Père-Lachaise cemetery, without finding her tomb." And do you know what she replied? "I'm afraid you are mistaken, my dear friend. I am dead, well and truly dead." Can you imagine?

Meanwhile, newcomers had integrated our strident but unanimous group. It frightened me. As for Gérard, he was smiling... He had started to walk again, and was soon almost running. I followed him. We went through the wall of singers, among which I thought I recognized a few regulars from the Café de Valois... And they were singing and singing. In the middle of that crowd, Gérard moved like a deep-sea fish. He was swimming. He was talking, talking to himself. I did my best not to lose him. I half-understood what he was saying.

- She is dead. It's a pity, we all agree. But what good can come out of all that moony desolation, I'm asking you? Well, truth, nothing but the truth: she ran away with my double. In reality, she never loved me. She only loved in me what she found that was similar to my double. Nothing else. By the way, have you seen the photograph Nadar took of me? Honestly, I don't recognize myself. It is not me. It can only be my double. Him, again! But who knows... I never actually met him. People I know very well saw him, even talked to him. Apparently he is not funny at all! But alas, he found favour with Jenny. They left together. They took the initiative! But not for long, do not worry yourself! I won't be long joining them, just to put some order into all that.

We stopped for a while. Gérard was looking straight ahead. I followed his gaze...

Jenny Colon was there... In front of us... She was smiling.

She was accompanied by a young man.

Gérard closed his eyes.

- It's him, it's my double... But they are dead, both of them. Dead, well and truly dead! Tell me when he's gone. You can't ignore that one should never look one's double in the eyes.

Meanwhile, a deadly silence prevailed around us. The singers had departed.

Jenny stared at me. The man who accompanied her had closed his eyes. Gérard was right: she was already dead... Or, at least, something in her was dead.

With a mocking smile, she walked away, singing: "I don't believe in love".

- Have they left? Gérard asked.

- He's no longer there.

- We had a lucky escape, he sighed. Just walking in the street has become a risk. A risk of death. Although death, you cannot ignore it, death is nothing but a detail.

I was looking around me. I was alone. Gérard had disappeared.

I carried on my way.

"Death is nothing but a detail."

I could hear Gérard's voice. It rang in my head like a nasty echo. It literally haunted me, and mingled with the words of Jenny Colon's lucky song, " Love is nothing but a detail".

I found myself in front of the Café de Valois. At this time, it was almost empty. The clock showed ten in the morning. Too early, too late. The journalists had already left, and the retired and the poets didn't begin to make their appearance until around 11 o'clock.

The agathopèdes' meeting had been fixed for ten thirty.

Gaston came with my coffee and my slice of bread and butter (half-salted).

The Count of Harambure lifted his head briefly from his newspaper to welcome me and re-immersed himself straight away into *La Quotidienne*. Robert Galland made an extremely discreet entrance. He ignored me and went to sit at a far table. He was elsewhere. The Marques of Rivarol entered without a fuss. Théodule Beau appeared, accompanied by Madame de Saint-Renaud. Others showed up too, in an aquatic silence.

I was waiting, at the same time as I was absolutely sure that no member of our brotherhood would show up. It often occurs that I feel alone in the world. Even now, after all these years of wandering in the territories of twilight. Even here, in the wasteland made of dark humidity that lives in me. Even in this moment, I feel myself the prey of solitude. But not a solitude caused by bitter disappointment, or the indifference of the world. No, it's something much more nasty: in that solitude which surrounds me, I feel, if I may say so, an upstart! Can you imagine? As if I didn't deserve that solitude, on top of it all! As if I was an impostor.

Time flew. I waited.

Then Gérard appeared. He greeted everyone discreetly. Everyone except me.

He was accompanied by a stranger, to whom he pointed at me with his finger, before sitting at his table. The stranger remained for a while watching me, I am tempted to say "contemplating me". I thought for a moment he was going to approach me (I hate that), but he suddenly appeared to change his mind, did a half-turn and went to sit at the back of the room.

Time moved with a suffocating slowness.

A waiter came to me.

- Monsieur Flanders, I'm sorry, it's all my fault! I omitted to tell you that your friends are waiting at the Café Lemblin. They decided to change location for the meeting at the last minute.

- Thanks, my friend, it's not that important.

- What do you mean, it's not that important? It's terribly important! Because of me you lost one hour of your time, one hour! I could never forgive myself.

- Tut tut, here's a little tip to comfort you...

- You are too good, Monsieur Flanders.

The Café Lemblin was not far away. "It is odd, though, to have chosen that centre of bohemian romanticism, I said to myself, that temple of bitterness and vain glory!" It didn't fit with our agathopedic condition. An agathopède has to practise severe frivolity, joyful stoicism, calculated inelegance. The complete opposite of the regulars at the Café Lemblin, where envy, morbid jealousy, the spirit of failure and vertigo of the fall prevailed... Otherwise, why would it be called "the Café of Icaruses"?

When I appeared in the main room, I was greeted with cheers and "It's him, it's the Man!"

When I sat down, a long silence followed.

- Who's going to tell him the news?

- Van Dame! This time he will be the spokesman for the Eternal.

Van Dame blushed (he always blushed). He stood up.

- Tonight again, as is the tradition, there will be a duel.

- That's what I understood at our last meeting.

- Yes, but as you were late, we drew the candidates and you are the winner.

- I am most honoured, I said, but I thought it was your turn, my dear Van Dame...

- Destiny has decided otherwise.

- I accept...

It was my turn, then. It had to happen some day. They all had been subjected to the same test. So why did I have those cold sweats, those shivers? Was I such a coward?

After that, we changed subject. We talked about inventing a catalogue of coins from the 17th century belonging to non-existent countries. In fact it was about imagining a new map of the world where France would share borders with Cathay and Siberia, where Portugal would have a border with the Ukraine and Columbia. We lost a few hours reinventing the world. Then, everyone left.

We had arranged to meet at the "bouchon Tellier" at eight on the dot.

- *I have an explanation*, a faceless voice said.

Did I mention already that one of the regular members of the brotherhood of the cryptesthesist spiritualists had no face? Always the first to sit at the table, this one. He said nothing. He was, in principle, forced to stay mute because of that lack, although it was without importance in his daily life. He didn't have a face... for me. In other words, he had a face, but "which didn't work". He was impervious to the turbulent tremors of the coming and going from one world to the next.

- *I have an explanation for that panic crisis*, the faceless man insisted.

- *Speak up.*

- *It is all very simple: our friend here knew he was going to die in that duel.*

- *That makes no sense,* Manfred said.

Manfred, on the opposite, had too much face. He owned an "uncertain" physiognomy. His protean face was forever sliding. Man, woman, young, old. All the races were displayed in turns on the characterless canvas that was his face.

- *I insist, it doesn't mean anything. Our friend is telling us the last day of the life that was his in the world he invented for himself. It is however clear as spring water that that world doesn't exist. It is nothing but a "cryptesthetic effect". Our friend doesn't exist, never did. He is nothing but a manifestation of the external brain of our medium.*

- *Solipsism!* The faceless man added.

- *The non-existence of Monsieur Flanders is just one of the hypotheses. It is possible he has a "separate" existence, what I am tempted to call "a threshold of life".*

- You claim he exists for real, next to the world, I mean, to our world?

- Next, around, entangled, the question is not about that. He has a diffuse existence. Like a character in a novel... No more no less. He has been created from nothing by ourselves. Yes, my friends, by ourselves! By the means of a transpersonal process, we are carrying our own daydreams, inventions, whims, you name it!

- Nonsense!

Everybody is talking at the same time. Yelling even.

It has set me thinking. There is a thing that's bothering me since I started evoking the deeds and misdeeds of my fugitive and flimsy life: I feel more and more that I'm living it again... For real, like a new thing... Like, if you want, something that has never been experienced. Earlier on, without going any further, I was actually living the meeting of the agathopèdes. I could see them. Do you understand? (I say "you" but I don't know whom I'm talking to.) And I felt a panic. It invaded me.

- Nonsense!

- I was already aware you were an idiot, but not to that degree, my dear. Allow me to be honest.

Again, everybody is talking at the same time.

- We are terminating the séance. We will examine all that next week, when calm has returned.

I find myself once again in the street. The weather is nice. Now I know I am living the last days of my life. I say farewell to all those faces, all those bodies. Each tree acknowledges me and says goodbye. They are all looking at me. They all "know".

Calm returns gradually. Panic will be followed by a kind of intoxication. And intoxication will make room for plethoric euphoria. And if, after all, I didn't die...? In principle, our duels terminate "when we draw blood".

I suddenly catch myself making plans for the future. Last time I met up with Houssaye, we discussed my soon-to-be engagement with that delicious Limenian I had been introduced to at Madame Cottard's home. I had found the thing unthinkable, but, facing "the Eternal", the nature of the thing changed. It was charged with a kind of fatal urgency.

I decided to pay an impromptu visit to my dear Arsène. His office was not far away.

I found him reading a voluminous manuscript.

- Those good people can no longer keep it brief. Life is brief, however they persist… They write endless novels. They want eternity and are convinced they can only conquer it by writing novels of an obesity worthy of Buddha. What can I do for you?

- I would have liked to invite you for lunch.

- With pleasure. Give me two minutes and I am yours.

Once the order was placed, Houssaye looks me straight in the eyes.

- You are not well. What is happening to you?

- Nothing, my dear friend, nothing special. I have to fight in a duel.

- With whom?

- I don't know.

- Your famous duels. I think it's stupid, if you want my opinion.

- Me too…

- So then! You shouldn't do it!

- Too late.

- Nonsense!

We eat our starters in silence. Then he gets back on his hobbyhorse.

- Mind you, I have nothing against long novels, as long as one has an adequate subject. Take the one I'm reading for the moment, for example. It's about a spectre. Why not? It unfolds during a séance. It is fashionable, I get it, I admit. The problem is, it goes in all directions: the ghost in question starts to tell his life. We learn he is Belgian, I know the writer did it on purpose, he knows I'm Belgian. He recounts his childhood in Ghent, his coming to Paris. He inflicts on us the gossips and malicious rumours of the little Parisian world. His (invented) love life. Of course he talks about the beautiful Limenian girl (by the way, we need to talk about her). Well, that's it really. Almost a thousand pages. Do you think it reasonable?

- Obviously not! Two hundred should have been sufficient.

- I am totally of that opinion too.

- And who is that writer?

- A so-called Coulage.

- Never heard of him.

- He is young, full of energy. But…

- But he is writing my story!

- How's that?

- He is telling my own story.

Houssaye remains silent for a while.

- Well well, that's true! I haven't thought about that. Obviously it is! I thought the story was vaguely familiar. Belgium, of course. Ghent, the father clockmaker, chemist. The two mad sisters... It's you!

- But how could he possibly do it? Is it about a desert rose?

- Well, yes.

- And a painter who is guided by the croaking of the frogs?

- Yes again. And of course it is about the agathopèdes.

Again he remains silent for a while.

- It is also about your death.

We spend the rest of the meal savouring our boeuf bourguignon in silence.

- Cheese? No? Coffee?

- Yes, a coffee please.

Again the silence settles comfortably between us.

- My death, you were saying?

- Yes, in the novel you die... Today, we are the 15th of June. You are supposed to die tonight. But it's only a novel, isn't it? Does it disturb you?

- Yes, it disturbs me... Tell me, on which page am I supposed to die?

- Let's see...

He leafs through the manuscript.

- You die exactly on page 170.

- Only!

- You said it! Because there are still two hundred pages in that first volume. And that's without counting the other two.

- And I disappear on page 170!

- Yes, but you reappear twenty pages further on! Just after your funerals. Which are, I mean will be, a real success, take my word. The Paris smart set will be there. The whole of the literary family! Musicians, painters, even some politicians. My congratulations, in advance.

- Thank you, but I am dead, nonetheless.

- But your spirit will survive you. You will be one of the most summoned up spirits in the most fashionable séances.

- At this moment?

- At this moment and in the future. A curious posthumous glory, my friend, well, according to the novel still. Your posthumous life will be endless, exactly like the novel.

Once again we bury ourselves in a tensed silence.

Houssaye asks for the bill and refuses to share it.

- No, I'm begging you! One cannot let the condemned man pay.

- And you find it funny…

- What do you want me to do about it?

As we leave, we shake hands for a long time, in silence, as if it's the last time.

- You have been warned, haven't you? Avoid duels.

- I promise.

The day is sunny. I stroll, leisurely and aimlessly. I linger at some bouquinistes on the quays.

One single idea, one fixed idea occupies my mind: how to avoid that duel everybody is waiting for?

And suddenly, I stop dead in my track: am I a complete idiot? I can easily decide to have dinner alone at Fabrice's. It's quite far from Paris. One eats well there, and it's reasonably priced. But above all, there is no danger out there. In any case, no danger of a fatal duel. Tomorrow I shall invent some excuse.

I look for a carriage, on the place du Châtelet.

- Do you take long rides?

- Not as far as the Valois, you know!

- Why do you say that?

- Because two weeks ago, your friend Nerval asked me to take him all the way to the Valois county.

- Did you refuse then….

- You must be joking! You don't refuse that. I probably earned more than in the whole of last year.

- That won't be the case this time.

- So let's go, we're on our way!

We leave Paris smoothly. I feel myself come back to life. I fall asleep, and dream about the duel. I wake up in a sweat.

- We are nearly there, the coachman announces.

Fabrice in person comes out to greet us.

- Willkommen, Signor Flanders. Your arrival was announced for tomorrow, but in the end it is as well you are here tonight, it's better. Tomorrow I'm having a wedding. And I know you like peace.

- It's the only thing I like.

- Exactly! Today, there won't be anyone. And I have something to offer you that will set you thinking.

- We'll see to that later, Fabrice. For now I need a room to have a wash and rest for an hour or so.

- Well that, on the other hand, will prove a bit difficult. My last available room has just been rented by a gentleman. A Belgian, just like you. But I can offer you my daughter's room. She has gone away for a while. She is in town and only comes back next week.

- Thank you Fabrice, I accept your offer. I am exhausted.

- You work too much.

- Not too much, don't believe that, but... You said a Belgian?

- Who's that? Oh, the gentleman... He claims he is from Belgium, indeed. A writer, like you.

- I am not a writer.

- Really! I was told you were.

- By whom?

- By... your fellow-countryman.

- The Belgian? Does he know me?

- Well, he is the one who announced you were arriving tomorrow.

- Is that so? You learn things every day.

It's odd, I feel more and more like I am living my memories. Like I'm being in a sharp, insistent present, painfully intense. And staggeringly slow. Sometimes I have the feeling I am living twice the events that befall me. Twice, but in a slightly different manner. Things move forward to immediately move backwards. And the segments of action are each time shorter, shorter and lighter.

I must have fallen asleep. One hour, two perhaps?

The bells of the church of Saint-Cloud are ringing eight o'clock.

When I go down to the dining room, the stranger is there. He looks at me without responding to my nod.

I order the *poularde à la flamande*.

- Like your comrade, Fabrice says.

- Ah. What a coincidence. And a bottle of house Bourgogne...

- Like him.

- And to start with, the salad of herrings and apples. Like him, perhaps?

- He didn't order a starter.

- Yes, says the other, who hasn't missed out on one bit of our conversation.

- Actually, I shall have the scrambled eggs with cèpes.

Then each buries himself in imponderable reflections.

What is happening to me? The memories are gradually becoming indiscernible from an unpredictable present. From a present that constantly evades me. Fragments itself. From which each atom, as if it had been thrown into panic, was (is) in the process of forming a kind of whirlwind where several other presents would co-exist.

We ate in a deadly silence, punctuated (precisely) by the church bells that called to a mass for the dead.

The stranger went to bed first, without bidding goodnight, without even looking at me.

I lingered at the table. Fabrice told me the village's latest gossip. But he especially talked about his daughter. She had a fiancé, the chemists' son, but Fabrice worried she might be in Paris with another man.

- If my suspicions are confirmed, I shall kill her. Yes, I shall. I prefer the guillotine to dishonour. You know, Monsieur Flanders, we Flemish people are like that. Honour is sacred, especially for someone like me. Let's not forget I went to Waterloo, didn't I?

He offered me a kummel that I accepted.

How many did we drink? Four, five glasses? When I went up to my bedroom, the church clock struck midnight.

I fell asleep almost immediately, without taking the trouble to undress myself.

At that present moment in my imperfect past, to dream is almost a pleonasm, a distortion in the muscular time of the revenants. In that time made of mechanical tensions and spiritual distensions. In that obscene mechanics "between two worlds": between today's world of mystical uniqueness and the plural world of yesteryear.

Besides, doesn't the word "revenant" leave you perplexed? What is it exactly, a revenant? A being that is forever coming back. And a so-called "living" being that doesn't stop becoming.

A pun? Not so sure.

But without going any further (further than what?), I, and it happens to me more and more (more of what?), I, when I come back, I become. And when I become, I come back. Which forces me to say forever "but this time, I am becoming", meaning living again in a different way what I already lived. Different? We will see. I am at Fabrice's because I want to avoid a duel that can only end badly, at least for me. If in spite of all there was a duel, or something similar, then one would have to face the facts that something like "fatality" would have happened. My refusal to accomplish what has already been written, or, if you wish, what has already been lived once and for all, will have dragged me to the realm of the "no difference to me".

All that to tell you that I'm sinking in a dream with no images, a dream with no stories.

Around four in the morning, a voice wakes me up.

- So it's him!...

- No, it's not him. There is no "him".

- You make me laugh! And what is he doing in your bed?

- I don't know. Perhaps my father has rented him my room. He was not expecting me before tomorrow. I don't know.

- You don't know!

- No, I swear.

- Bitch!

At that moment, I intervene.

- Listen, Monsieur, Mademoiselle told you the truth: Fabrice rented me her room for one night.

- And you want me to believe you!

- Beware! I don't like to be on familiar terms with a complete stranger!

I get up and slap him.

A long silence tries to settle, but I break it without scruples.

- Will you kindly leave my room.

- "My room"! He says "my room"? All right, I accept leaving the room but not without your charming company.

In the end, there will be a duel, after all.

We go out.

- We are going to fight, that goes without saying, but with what?

- I always travel with two pistols, just in case.

- A wise precaution, I add.

The young woman just fainted. We no longer pay her any attention. Suddenly, only the duel matters. We place ourselves twenty paces apart.

Pistol fire. A single shot.

The young man collapses without a word.

Then Fabrice comes out of the shadow.

- That's a good thing done, he says.

The young woman wakes up.

- Are you all right, Aline?

- I'm fine, father. And thank you for getting rid of that man for me. He had become a real nightmare.

- It's all right, daughter. We are going to bury him in the garden, under the pear tree. Our friend Flanders will give us a hand.

- That goes without saying.

The dirty job keeps us busy for an hour or so.

Then we drink a coffee accompanied by a liqueur from Alsace. Life is beautiful.

Day breaks. Aline keeps us company. In silence. Not a single comment on what has just happened. She is beautiful. Extremely beautiful.

The bells announce that the first mass of the day is about to begin. We decide to attend. We will take the opportunity to pray for the soul of the stranger.

- Now that he is no longer with us, you can occupy his room.

- Good idea.

Alone in my room, in his room, I rummage through his things. A shirt, a map of the region. A drawing, undoubtedly made last night, attracts my attention. The man has drawn a map of Fabrice's garden. There is a circle marked with an arrow.

The pear tree.

He has marked in advance the spot where we buried him!

I start reading:

"I was born the very day my father died in a duel. That could have been just an incident, an accident, a subject of conversation to liven up mournful evenings, so frequent in the provinces. Alas! My father's death in a duel marked all the events of my life, even the most insignificant. At that precise moment when I let my quilt pen glide over the paper, yes, even now, I "see" my father dying… I hear his last words: "Tell my son that I thought about him at the supreme moment." It is true that to die in a duel killed by one's own brother, as our late lamented Henri used to say, " is not ordinary". Indeed! His brother killed him… To be killed by one's own brother was not ordinary… But the reason was. A lady."

I stopped reading… There was something else that was not ordinary either: the writing. It was mine!

- What do you mean by that?

It all disappears again. I am back at my dear cryptesthetists, right in the middle of a séance.

- There is something wrong. Our friend has committed a few discrepancies. For a start, he has decided to change the date and circumstances of his death.

- For our enjoyment.

- That's true, but nevertheless.

- Admit all he said is exciting.

- True, again.

- Furthermore, he is in line with our theory.

- What do you mean?

- It is obvious that, from all the things he said, it follows that the subject is a pure invention of our medium!

- And of ourselves.

I keep quiet. I must confess that the idea of being solely the medium's invention has left me thinking.

- I propose for our friend to go back on his childhood memories.

- I totally agree.

- Yes, yes. Personally, I didn't go beyond his stay in England.

- I love the sisters.

- As far as I'm concerned, I would have liked him to narrate the good and bad fortune of his return to Paris the day after his announced death.

- Me too.

- What do we do? Shall we vote?

I'm beginning to get impatient.

- I am not a storyteller, by the way. It's my life, my own life! And it's not my fault if I wanted to escape my death. It's called the instinct of self-preservation!

- You claim not to be a storyteller, but you are telling us stories! We did some research. And we found things. We know you died in a duel.

- I've told you so already.

- And we took the trouble to check your stories.

- On the other hand, your journey to Fabrice's…

- That is another story. Another story altogether.

- Tell us that.

- Let's see… I think I spent a good part of the day reading the manuscript my unfortunate rival was writing when death took him.

Again I find myself on the spot, it is therefore not memories. I am surrounded by a present world, too present. I am living another life. A complement of life in the aftermath of the duel. How to explain that? How to evoke the aromas rising from the kitchen to my room? It is not a memory, it's life experience. I am in a present of a dizzying presence (you can say that again). That present is like an external world that would reveal itself to be more internal, more subjective than the self that is submitted to it. I know all that has no meaning, but the thing is real, too real.

I read, I discover a character with whom I have several things in common. First, his Belgian-ness. He spent his childhood in Ghent. He speaks about his mother's hotel. He describes the market… For a moment, I thought I recognised myself in that boy he meets in the streets and who, seeing him, runs away as if he had seen a ghost.

I have lunch with Fabrice and his daughter. How gorgeous she is! I cannot take my eyes of her. And she is not insensitive to me as I gaze at her. And all that cannot escape the piercing gaze of Fabrice. I dream, I float!

Suddenly, a kind of panic seizes me by the throat. Shivers. I say to myself: "I must have died yesterday evening in Paris, what am I doing here?" But that "here", my God, is so breathtaking! Again, I experience that sensation of being inhabited by a present made of too many things, in which I no longer succeed in making a way for myself. I am in a world that is more personal than myself, perhaps I should say "ultra-personal".

After lunch, I go up to my room and carry on reading. I reach the page where a certain Flanders, an agathopède (therefore me) is killed by the narrator, the one who is now lying under the pear tree. I resume my reading… But I grow tired of it. The prose is deadly boring, full of useless details and so-called "philosophical" reflections. It's all nonsense.

There is a knock on my door. It is her.

- Can I?

- Come in, please!

She sits down and looks at me silently for quite a while.

- It's all very sad. He is dead and it's my fault. I made him jealous, do you understand? I played with his feelings. I am unforgivable.

- No, no, you have nothing to do with it. If there's someone to blame, it is me.

- No, not you.

Another silence. It continues. Suddenly she gets up.

- There is a solution. A single one. But which?

She says that as if it was a fact.

- But which?

Another silence, nastier still, more insidious. Then she speaks. It seems she has changed her voice. It sounds like a man's voice. And I recognize that voice, but from where?

- We need to get married.

- What?

- You and me. Married. My father agrees.

- What do you mean?

- It's him who sent me.

- Married?

- Married!

- I fear it all feels a bit rushed!

- It's as good as done. My father has sent for the priest and the mayor. The ceremony will be held next week. I am really sorry that thing has taken you by surprise.

A third silence settles.

- She is so damn gorgeous…

- That's not enough, my dear (it's a voice I've already heard, a moment ago, and now I recognize it: it's the voice of the young man who died a few hours before).

Yes, she is beautiful, too beautiful. Yes, I said it already and I shall say it again, I'll exaggerate on purpose. Beautiful, beautiful again.

And the voice, again, the voice of the young man:

- What is so extraordinary about that young lady? Neither tall nor small, sad eyes but sparking; neither fat nor skinny, in a word, the type of woman Mérimée described as "neither nor". Yes, said Prosper, Carmen didn't have anything extraordinary about her, at first sight. She was borderline "ordinary". If one divided her body parts into "yes" and "no", the people of Seville would have said she had five "yes" and twelve "no", but that her "no" was, and by far, more beautiful than the "yes" of the other women from Seville.

We all agreed to fix the ceremony two weeks from then. It was going to spark off some gossips, but the hell with that.

That same evening, I went back to Paris. I walked straight into the Café de Valois.

On seeing me, Gaston turned back and went to seek refuge in the kitchen. A few minutes later, he reappeared, accompanied by the owner and his daughter.

They couldn't believe their eyes.

- We thought you were no longer from this world.

- I know. But I am here, I said.

- It looks like it.

- But then, the duel... the comments... Today you were on everybody's lips, the suicide of the Duke of Fagès passed into second place; the murder of Prince Pelletier...

- I hope my death made you sad.

- Of course!

I sat down at my usual table. My colleagues were about to arrive. The first to do so was Matras, the only Parisian in the group. He stared at me for a while, with no expression on his face, as someone who, indifferent, looks at a cow galloping. He sat at a table opposite mine, but showed me his back. Then it was Orlac's turn. It was worse, he went to sit opposite Matras, without a single glance towards me. Two minutes later, the extravagant Schwarzbrucke made a noteworthy entrance, but not worth it: he thought it was a good idea to do a few dance steps while uttering little, imperceptible moans.

One by one, the eight Parisian agathopèdes took possession of the two tables. And none, not a single one, deemed it necessary to even glance at me briefly. I didn't exist. However, Gaston had recognized me! And the owner, and his daughter.

I called Gaston.

- My dear Gaston, would you be so kind as to act as the go-between between those good agathopèdes and myself?

- There is no use, Monsieur Flanders, they think you are dead.

- What do you mean?

- Or rather, they are annoyed to see you here safe and sound.

- But surely they should be happy, shouldn't they?

- That's also my opinion. But you know your agathopèdes better than I do, don't you? They are vexed because it will be reported that your death is another prank by the agathopèdes. And a prank is prepared with meticulous care. An involuntary prank is more than moronic, it is abject.

- What does it all mean! I am not dead, full stop.

- I agree with you, but that's how they are.

Matras called Gaston.

I remain perplexed. I am telling my story for a while. I mean to say I remember and no longer am in the heart of the event. Events come to me because I evoke them. They draw near me with an almost threatening nonchalance. The scene at the Café de Valois painfully emerges. That is no longer something experienced, it is memories.

I ask for another coffee. I need to repeat my order.

But that coffee doesn't taste the same. It seems to have no taste. No taste at all.

And the agathopèdes are laughing. At some point, I hear my name mentioned.

- Flanders? Orlac says... Oh, him!

- Well, let's say he was not really up to it, Matras replies.

- It could have been worse, Scharzbrucke retorts.

Then someone, Villers perhaps, says:

- Let him rest in peace.

There is a long silence.

There was a long silence.

It is obvious: they are waiting for a reaction on my part. I stand up, I walk with some kind of liturgical solemnity towards their tables. The customers in the café are taking it all in, each of my movements. They are expecting the worse. And I cannot disappoint them.

- Messieurs, I shall wait for you at the Tuileries, precisely opposite. One by one and one after the other. I leave you with the honour of choosing the order of arrival.

- When blood is drawn, I guess? Orlac says.

- You decide.

I left in no hurry. I could feel their mocking gazes following me.

I waited for them quietly, smoking an Abdullah. I must have waited a good hour. Nobody came! It's true nothing had been prepared, no weapons, no witnesses, not even the reasons for the duel. But that cavalier way they slipped away! I would never have thought that, especially from a gentleman, what's more, an agathopède.

I went back to the café. They had all left by the service entrance. Like thieves!

And I was still there, still alive.

I walked back to my apartment on rue de l'Ancienne-Truanderie.

I met two or three neighbours, we said good evening… They could see me, that was better than nothing. At home, I found Madame Ménard. She was about to leave.

- Ah, it's you. I thought you were in the countryside. Your friends came to fetch you.

- What friends?

- Your agathopèdes!

- I beg your pardon? When was that?

- About an hour ago.

- But an hour ago they were in the same café as me!

- Or half an hour. Do you want me to tell you my impression? They were up to something. I don't know, a prank. They stayed on the staircase, talking for a while. I heard something that stayed in my head: "We are going to pretend he doesn't exist… we are going to persuade him he died in the duel he wanted to avoid."

- I see.

- Did they do it?

- Yes…

- Then they are not friends. A friend, a true one, doesn't do that.

- They did it.

So my agathopède brothers were nastier that I thought. They were odious, cruel.

- Come on now, don't think about it too much, mother Ménard said, they are being childish.

She left. I went upstairs to lie down.

Again, I saw myself climbing the stairs. I was floating around myself. I saw myself getting undressed. I was stuck to the ceiling and could see myself down there. And it looked like my image, my body could see me. It was staring at me.

In the end, he fell asleep. At the same time, I fell on myself, and I plunged into the darkness.

The day after, I got up early and went out for a short walk. The garden of the Tuileries was delightful. I probably met twenty or so acquaintances. Only three pretended not to see me.

I felt reassured.

I decided to pay a visit to Houssaye.

The main door was open. I went in. A secretary whom I knew well because there had been something between us, walked past me without saying good morning. She closed the door and disappeared into her office. Either she hadn't seen me, or she bore a lasting grudge against me.

Arsène, on the contrary, received me with open arms.

- Very, very happy to see you safe and sound. You were absolutely right to escape such a pointless and meaningless duel. Those idiotic ceremonies must be stopped. Idiotic and dangerous. Only yesterday evening, there were three deaths! No, we can't carry on like that!

We had lunch again together. Arsène was inexhaustible. He spoke, and spoke: the barricades, the murders on the rue Saint-Merri, Nerval's travels. I listened.

I hear him... I can still hear him.

He left me in front of the Théâtre du Châtelet. I saw him walking off with quick steps, then stopping before someone I had known in the past then lost sight of. Arsène talked to him, pointing at me. The other let him hold forth by himself, and came rushing to me. He stopped a few metres from me and contemplated me at length. Without any friendliness, but without any antipathy either. I said to myself: "I shall never forget that look." He said nothing, but I felt his gaze noisy like a tavern at midnight. He yawned in front of me. And there was hatred in that yawning.

- Good day, I said.

- Good day.

But I heard a woman's voice behind me:

- You will always surprise me, my dear friend. I thought we were no longer on speaking terms.

- That's true. Between you and me, there's nothing left. It's finished.

- Why then say "Good day"? the woman whom I couldn't see continued.

- I was under the impression that someone, not you, had said Good day to me.

- Oh, really! Like that! You said "someone".

- Someone who remains invisible to us. For the time being.

- Good day, I said, to fill the silence that was becoming stifling.

He answered with a "Good day", dry and barren.

- Well, you persist!

- Sorry, but someone said Good day to me.

- Who, then? The invisible man still?

- Still.

Suddenly, they walked off together. I was left alone. I didn't really know what to think. They could hear me but they could no longer see me. There was cause for alarm.

I spent the rest of the day strolling. I went from bank to bank. I probably came across around ten acquaintances. Half responded to my greetings.

The day after, it was Gaston's turn. Even him, even Gaston could no longer see me. In the staircase of my apartment building, nobody saw me.

Three days later, there was no one left who could see me. That at least was how it seemed to me.

In a rush I produced a dozen hypotheses. Gradually I accepted the easiest one: it was undoubtedly a conspiracy. An agathopède prank. They wanted to drive me insane.

I decided to leave. At least, at Fabrice's, I would meet up with my beloved. And be met with good food.

Alas, there were several surprises in store for me.

First, I couldn't find a single carriage prepared to drive me there. The coachmen didn't see me. They could hear me, of course. They looked around, scratching their heads. Nodding. It was hilarious! On the other hand, the horses could see me. And I frightened them. They went into a frenzy, poor things. One even set off at a trot, leaving the coachman stranded on the pavement!

After lunch, I returned home. I had (I have) two or three things to settle before going back to my beloved.

- Oh, those disgusting ashes!

A great burst of laughter followed...

- Who said that?

I look around me. Nothing. I am alone in my room. But, is it my room? That wardrobe, those chairs? In any case, that room where I was spending the night was not there before, as far as I know. And the window didn't look out over the square.

Where am I?

I experience again the sensation of a present. A present that would be tracing my memories.

I leave my room. In front of me, a long corridor whose end is lost in the darkness... There is no ceiling, it looks like a starry sky... I think I see flying objects whose flashing frightens me.

I open another door and find myself right in the middle of an avenue. On each side, huge buildings swallow up English-speaking crowds with a gargantuan appetite. Someone approaches me and welcomes me in French. I recognize the Marseille accent of the stranger from the place du Châtelet. I retrace my steps. Once again I am in the dark corridor. And this time, I recognize it. It's well and truly my corridor. Finally I am back in my world. I recognize it. I enter my room. Everything is in its place.

Except for that stranger.

- Who are you?

He stares at me, looking as surprised as I am.

- Who are you? he says.

- Me? I'm in my home, of course!

- Me too, I'm in my home, of course!

I take some time recognizing my double. He is me, or I am him.

One would think we were at Hoffman's place.

- Sit down, please.

- Thank you, but I'm in a hurry.

- Me too, I'm in a hurry.

- Really! But not for the same reasons as I am.

- I don't know your reasons.

- I don't know yours.

- Mine are not a secret... I'm about to get married in two weeks time and I want to pay a visit to my beloved.

- Me too.

The other looks at me, without saying a word.

- You mean to say we love the same woman?

- It looks like it...

- It is impossible. Or rather, it is intolerable...

- I am at your disposal.

Who is who? Who says what?

- I shall send you my witnesses this very evening.

- Why wait?

- You are impatient.

- Are you not?

A third person appears.

- What are you two doing in my room?

A second double.

It all gets on my nerves.

- Too much is too much!

- Well, really! How's that, "too much"?

A fourth person manifests himself. And a fifth and a sixth.

Everybody speaks at the same time.

I take advantage of the confusion to run away. I am alone in the street. I run, and run. When I arrive at the Châtelet, surprise, surprise: they are there. All of them. How many? Twenty, thirty, or more arguing over the carriages.

- To Fabrice's! To Fabrice's!

They all want to go to Fabrice's. They all have the same fiancée.

I turn round and leave.

An odd thing was happening to me: I was not surprised by what was happening to me. As in dreams, nothing surprised me. And again, I was not there: I was remembering. All those things had happened to me, a long time ago... Or never.

A voice brought me back to the present.

- You too want to go to Fabrice's?

- Yes, why?

For a moment or two, a carriage was following me.

- Climb in, I'll take you there.

- Gladly, even if I know that I shall arrive last.

- That's not sure. You will see.

And here we are, shaking off the other carriages, the districts fading behind us as if we were flying!

- What is it, that thing? A fancy dress ball?

- To be honest, I don't know.

- I am not surprised. I've seen all sorts.

- Why do you say "fancy dress ball"?

- You are all dressed the same. Is it on purpose?

- Not for me. To be honest, I don't know really.

We arrived first. And when I say first, I mean first: at Fabrice's, there was no one.

- How much do I owe you, Monsieur? I say to the coachman.

- Nothing, it's already paid for.

- Really, and by whom?

- I'm not allowed to tell you.

- But surely you won't refuse a tip, will you? You deserve it.

- Not even that.

The carriage left and I remained all alone.

All alone? Not so sure. There must have been someone in the vicinity, I could feel it. Someone whose eyes didn't leave me. What eyes? That's another story. How's that, "another story"?

Too many questions. Way too many questions. Questions? More likely, answers. I knew them, those famous answers without question that my dear agathopèdes were so fond of. Orlac always used to say: "It is absolutely necessary to give priority to answers. After, we will still have time to fabricate questions made to measure." Which annoyed Matras no end: "Nonsense! An answer without a question is like an egg without a hen!" Orlac's turn: "An egg without a hen is like a song without a voice!" And Schwarzbrucke's next: "A fart without an ass!" And so forth.

I was alone before the inn. No Fabrice. No beloved.

- And especially, no doubles!

Where was that voice coming from? I looked around. Somewhere, someone was sniggering.

- Who's there?

- I'm coming back.

- Is that true?

- It is bound to be true.

I let it drop. I was no longer counting the miracles.

- A horizon of miracles surrounds you, the voice of the invisible sniggering being replied.

- One will have to conclude that it's all miracles.

- It is the same as saying that there are no longer any miracles, Orlac's distant voice retorted.

There was a warm wind, which brought me back to the present. To which present? I was breathing deeply. I had lungs! I was in the present again. But it was a present, let's say, subjective, weakened by anxiety, which, in my own case, took the form of a nervous breakdown. In that kind of storm, one could find everything. A real junk room: first of all, euphoric flashings, fireworks that proclaimed with voices of castrati: "Life is beautiful", then feline purring that quietly said: "That's not sure", finally distant yawning that whispered: "Does it matter?"

A truly consensual bric-à-brac. Consensual and mean.

I was alone, that's all there is to it.

- And it didn't cross your mind to simply think: "Perhaps I am dead"?

The voice woke me up in a completely different present. The séance continued. I was still there. Surrounded by cryptesthetists bent on proving my non-existence.

- The medium is tired. We will have to terminate the séance.

- The medium is not tired.

- But look at her, dear colleague! She is exhausted. She is so pallid!

- She is always like that.

- Are you all right, Madame? Can we carry on?

- We can.

- We could perhaps return to our subject's childhood.

- Listen, I've had enough of your interruptions! Let the subject talk freely.

It all disappears.

I am again at Fabrice's, before the inn.

Here comes a carriage, then another, and another. How many? Eight, ten? Impossible to tell, it didn't stop. I saw myself surrounded by my doubles. They stared at me with a nasty, twisted look.

- Come on, please, why are you waiting to take action?

- Take action? What do you mean by that?

Fabrice appeared, coming out of nowhere.

- That's it, he said, this time you won't get away with it!

- Why not? And get away with what, precisely?

My beloved arrived. She was smiling. At the beginning, I thought she was looking at me. Then I said to myself: no, she is squinting. Finally I had to face the facts: she didn't see me! No one could see me. They were aiming at someone slightly to my left.

- Well, well. Are you going to fight, or not?

- Out of the question! First of all, with whom?

- With me, of course!

- Or me.

- Or me, without going any further.

- I take the liberty of informing you that you have invited us to go to the meadow.

- Yesterday, without going any further.

- Further from what, for god's sake!

- Here, we are already far enough.

I couldn't believe my eyes: my doubles were in the process of "transforming" their faces. They had become, one after another, the agathopèdes. The ineffable agathopèdes. More agathopèdes than ever. I had "invited" them, as they said, and they had come, my very dear guests of stone.

And each had his sword. Suddenly, that weight in my right hand. I had no more excuses.

The first duel began. Quickly started, quickly finished: blood was drawn.

The second was harder to conclude. My right hand was wounded. The third, fourth, fifth were endless.

I was exhausted.

We had a pause.

Fabrice offered us a light meal, cold chicken accompanied by a bottle of Chablis. We ate in silence.

After half an hour, the fights started again.

With how many agathopèdes did I have bouts? After a dozen, I ceased counting.

Night was falling. An icy wind rose.

Torches were brought.

I carried on, still not counting. The wind blew out the torches.

We kept going in the darkness.

Suddenly lights appeared. It was Fabrice again, accompanied by three servants bearing new torches.

- Well, it has all gone too far, we should stop now, Adelin said.

Fabrice had prepared a sumptuous dinner, worthy of a king's table: carps, woodcocks, a leg of lamb. Everyone talked ruthlessly. The quick chat sparkled with such a healthy euphoria that it sounded like a Chinese cemetery. Celebration and sorrow.

Nobody talked to me. At the beginning I didn't notice. But when I joined in the conversation, my words crashed against a wall of silence. As I insisted, with the excuse of having something important to say, I was met with an unanimous laughter that burst like chimes. Then I had to face the facts: I was a burden in this world. I had become a troublemaker.

By chance, there was a moment of silence. I took advantage of it.

- My friends, I said, my very dear friends, we are all going to die....

- Hold on! What is he talking about!

- We are all going to die. But beware, after this life, there will be a follow-up... And it will be a ferocious follow-up. Ferocious and dull.

- Dull? Explain yourself, or we will sadly have need to take to duels once again.

- What does it matter, I'm already dead.

- What is he talking about? Would there be a life after death?

- Yes!

- Have you become a believer? Arnim exclaimed. In that case, I would kindly invite you to leave.

- No and no! That's enough! For the moment we are eating.

- Yes, dear friends, there is a life after death. I am in the right place to tell you that, for I come from there. At this very moment, I am recounting what you are experiencing.

- But if you are dead, how come we can see you?

- And hear you. Although I have to confess I no longer recognize your voice.

- Because you are as dead as I am.

- Surely he is drunk!

- Yes, my friends. I, too, took time to realise our situation. But make an effort and you could like me, look in the face, courageously, that extreme oddity that consists in living again "for real", our historic past.

A lasting silence settled in the dining room. Then Matras spoke.

- Our friend here is right. I can also remember this very situation. I know: I know perfectly well that this situation has never happened in the past. I am making it up. Imagining it. And, by pure chance, I imagined the same thing as our friend Flanders. Exactly the same thing!

Another silence. Orlac spoke.

- Me too, he said. Me too, I come from there. At this very moment, I remember. I remember and I recount.

- Me too, Riguer, Saulnier and Védrine said.

- We are all in it together.

- You perhaps, but not me!

It was Fabrice talking.

- Wait a minute! I'm not sure you realise the privilege the Eternal had granted us, Saulnier said.

- Yes, I know, I know, Vedrine retorted with his usual spleen, we are all dead, and, by a strange coincidence, someone (you call him "the Eternal", I, more soberly, am tempted to give him the name of "genie of darkness") is playing a sinister game with us.

- I agree with you, Saulnier riposted. Nevertheless, he has catapulted us all simultaneously to Fabrice's for a dinner and a few duels (rather quirky, I have to admit), giving us the possibility for this last encounter.

- As well as the possibility, perhaps, to start a new life again, Riguer whispered, always the optimist.

- But how original could that life be to deserve to be called "new"? Vedrine said.

- And "renewable"?

A storm broke out in the distance. It sounded like an ovation, a stampede, an unanimous sneeze.

We stood up straight, and each took up an exaggerated pose.

The storm was approaching. The lightning flashes became more and more frequent. Increasingly rapid. Two, three, twenty times per second (or more).

I looked at my comrades, so fragile, so bravely frail...

Then they all disappeared into space.

I remained alone.

No Fabrice, no agathopèdes, my beloved impossible to find.

Again I experienced that sensation of a present. Of a present in the present. Of several presents fitted together, like Chinese boxes.

I was there in more than one way, and at the same time. Enough to amaze the impassive Védrine.

- You see? said a voice I recognized straight away. You see how things are!

- I see nothing, nothing at all, I said.

- But at least you see me, don't you?

I could see him. Yes, no doubt about it... The young man of the pear tree, the hanged man, the dead and buried, the victim of a lost bullet. The man whose jealousy was fastidious and honour, pernickety, was there.

He was smiling at me.

- You will have to get used to it, he said, turning his back on me.

- It's been a while since I've been fazed by anything, in fact.

- Bad, very bad, he said. When I say you have to get used to it, I mean to say you shouldn't let yourself go... Not at all. Or you run the risk of becoming the plaything of mad genii, as Nerval would say. One has to master the thing. Tame the beast! In one word, one has to stay calm.

- For someone who still belonged to the world of the living barely a week ago, you show much experience, I said.

- But I still belong to the world of the living, beware of appearances! And you too, my friend, you too. Perspectives have changed, that's true! As we see things from a different angle, we lose sight of some, but we see others, that's all. No need being worked up about it, is it?

A carnivorous noise made me jump: next to me, Orlac was devouring a stuffed lamb shoulder.

It was obvious he couldn't see us.

- Here's an example, the young man of the pear tree said, he is there and he is not there.

A ball exploded and Matras came in through the window... The whistling of a thief, it was Schwarzbrucke. One by one, all the members of our brotherhood appeared, and each announced his appearance with an emblematic noise...

The banquet was in full swing. They were all there. Except me.

I was elsewhere. In an elsewhere close by but unreachable.

- I'm terribly sorry about it, but I can't do anything. I have to say they cannot see me either.

- Let's leave here. Would you like to go for a walk?

The night was beautiful. We went deep into the forest.

Gradually, as we went further away from the inn, the forest became darker and darker, more threatening. More carnal too.

The man of the pear tree was walking, hands in his pockets. From time to time his motionless legs became rigid. And, how should I say... shivers agitated them. Trembling, discreet, of course, but also real jolts.

He moved without walking, like a possessed man in a trance.

- Tell me, do you think one should believe absolutely everything one sees?

I looked at him. I noticed without surprise that he spoke without moving his lips.

- What do you mean by "believe"?

- Well, we've just seen with our own eyes a scene taken from a dream, isn't that so?

He had said "with our own eyes": his were closed.

I thought: several times it happened that I imagined human beings with whom I enjoyed talking for hours ("light-hours"). It even happened to be part of other people's daydreaming, one or several, in isolation or all together... But never ever did I end up in that situation of being part of the mental space of another person, and vice-versa.

That parallel dream drew us towards the softest, the most slimy area of the forest.

The most voracious too.

- You see, he said, your friend Orlac is right: we had the rare privilege of being present at the meeting of the dead agathopèdes a long time ago, dead and forgotten.

- It's sad.

- Do you think so? Do you really think so?

- Can a revenant believe?

- Just for New Year's Eve...

- For a second...

- It makes you wonder...

- Yes, yes.

Who was talking? Was he? Was I? Or was "he", that kind of composed self?

He, fourth person singular.

I looked at him.

He had mislaid, during the conversation, his left hand and his right ear.

Thus a revenant could decompose too... Can a ghost divide, and if he can, into how many parts?

- Forty-eight, he said silently (he had just mislaid his mouth).

What about me? How many parts of me had flown away to other astral bodies?

- To go back to our agathopèdes, I suspect an external force to have caused, approved and provoked this encounter in this so particular beyond.

- God?

- Something of that kind...

- There, you are taking us in areas that are beyond me.

- Did you ever hear people say: "We need a Bonapartism without Bonaparte"?

- You mean.... a deism without God?

- Or rather, why not, men like you and me. In a not so distant future.

- I see... Humans who, at this precise moment, are listening to us...

- Who are watching us.

- The inhabitants of the polar region.

- Do you see what I mean?

- Alas, yes.

- Amazing, isn't it?

- Alas, again.

- Men and women like you and me, but who suffer a penury, a kind of penury.

- Imagination, that they lack.

- That's it. But I find it difficult to understand which type of imagination they are talking about.

- Alas! Having no imagination, not at all, they cannot know.

- Blind people, in a way.

- You don't know how much you are speaking the truth…

- That's what I thought I understood.

- They are not capable of knowing what happened last year, last week. To visit the past, memory is powerless. One needs imagination.

- One imagines the past?

- I am absolutely convinced of that. Everything that happens to us, we imagine it, not in the same way. As for them, they are forced to construct a past from an outline.

- Which type?

- Good question. A temporal outline, they would say.

- There is a word that comes back repeatedly: "statistics"…

- What does that mean?

- A kind of "bet".

- Too complicated for me.

- Me? Did you say "me"?

- For example.

I could no longer see him. He had become sun dust.

In the middle of the night. A full moon night.

The wind scattered the dust and with it, our bodies.

- Where are you?

- Precisely where you are.

- Odd that you are there. I am nowhere.

- Nowhere or everywhere?

- We are agathopèdes again.

We carried on our ethereal walk. In the distance, I caught sight of Fabrice's inn… We could hear the voices of the agathopèdes. They were singing the hymn of our brotherhood: *La Bastonnade*.

How can I explain to you, how can I convey the feeling of absence I experienced as I approached the inn. Imagine you are living an everyday situation, an ordinary one, with nothing particular about it, like ambling along, for example. Ambling along in the forest, accompanied by someone in the habit of appearing and disappearing into the air, apparently without doing it on purpose. Imagine you are doing the same, your appearances and disappearances, let's say pendulous, teasing one another. From that teasing, enough to set one's mind on edge, emerges a kind of non-place, at the same time presence and absence. Worse: an event present *because absent*.

I am living this situation presently, I mean. However, it escapes constantly, becomes at times memory, at times prophecy.

- Don't lose time, your speculations are protecting themselves. They are running away, hiding behind that jungle of alibis.

- Jungle of alibis! Really you are exaggerating, my friend!

- Alibis of eternity.

- Now, really!

- It all happens in a kind of suspended present, doesn't it? A present that evolves in a loop.

- So?

- So you have the very distinct impression of living "next to the present". We are living all that, but we are living it "next to". It is a detached present. Detached and shifted. Is it clear to you?

- No.

Here we are in front of the window overlooking the banqueting hall. The hymn was drawing to its conclusion.

- Things end sometimes, my companion said, it is reassuring.

- What, my friend?

- This song…

- What song?

- All right, all right!

The scene discreetly evaporated. I was again staring at a ouija board.

- Well, we have to admit we strayed a bit from the subject that occupies us.

- Not us, him.

- It amounts to the same thing.

- Not at all, gentlemen, not at all!

- Our friend is making inhuman efforts to share with us his tribulations as a dead man…

- And he really believes that philosophy will resuscitate him?

- At least he's trying to die for good…

They talk, they talk and nobody listens. Suddenly I turn my back and leave.

I go down the stairs.

My celestial tramp is there. It looks like he is waiting for me.

- Long journey, eh?

- I no longer know, I'm losing my sense of time.

- I don't have that impression, I see you there, opposite me, and I can see your time.

- If you can see it, it means it no longer is mine, my "time". It is next to me.

- That's slightly true. But what else? Everything's okay? I mean, the people of the South Pole.

- It's all right.

- Have you already started?

- Not entirely, but it's taking shape…

- Did they ask you to tell your life?

- An "imaginary" life.

- Imaginary? And what did you answer?

- Well! I probably don't have much imagination. I invented the life of someone not very different from myself.

- That's what they wanted, isn't it?

- Not really. I invented myself "Belgian".

- You are already Belgian.

- Precisely. My imaginary double was born in Ghent.

- You were born in Ghent.

- Exactly! I was born in 1805. Therefore I am five years older than my double.

- That's already something.

- I am a painter.

- Like yourself.

- I discovered my vocation late in life. At the age of thirty, I was working for the Warburg bank. Then, from one day to the next, I abruptly decided to devote my life to painting.

- And you had three children, and your wife was Danish.

- Well, you are quite in the know, aren't you!

- Let me guess. You had a Dutch friend, a painter, like you.

- Well, yes, and we had an argument.

- About an ear.

- No, a finger. He cut his own finger. Besides, he gave it to me as a present, his finger.

- Why did you imagine all that?

- I don't know. It came to me like that... Higgledy piggledy.

- That story really happened. But later. After your death. In that story, you are called Paul, Paul Gauguin.

- Paul? No, my borrowed name is Marian, Marian Poirier.

- How old were you when you died?

- Forty.

I was saying anything and everything. I was cheating! And my tramp, he knew it, he had realised. And he was letting me go on. He found it amusing.

- Go on, tell me. Let's see if you are able to stick the pieces together.

- I was, I am Belgian. I am a writer.

- Writer of one single book, I guess.

- I, "he" writes the story of a so-called Flanders.

- Yourself.

- Myself. In fact.

- What about your bosses, what do they say?

- They ask questions, like you. They want details. It seems that's the only thing they are interested in. Yesterday, well, earlier, I mean in a moment, I must have lost a whole year describing a pair of shoes. The shoes Théophile Gautier was wearing the day of the "scarlet evening" at Madame de Genlis.

- Did you manage to do it?

- I made it up. I knew the two shoes were slightly different. It was enough as a starting point.

- You are smart. But that's a lot of work, nevertheless.

- No need to tell me!

Yes, at the beginning, it appeared so easy: "You are going to invent a life for our enjoyment", a whole life. In reality, I was asked to invent myself. A new life. I was spoilt for choice... I could tell my life as the emperor of China. Or as a Roman legionary, a Catalan bandit, I don't know! In fact, I was lucky: I invented my own life, with a slight shift. I was not to know that that life, I was going to live it. For real! I hadn't understood that each detail made up condemned me to live it... For real! That the death I narrated to them, I would have to suffer it. Literally (if I dare say so). But I thought I knew the reason for my insistence on going deep into the most minute details. I wanted to live again the life that had been mine, but with a slight shift. I wanted to see myself living it. I wanted to be the privileged witness to my real deeds and misdeeds. And above all I wanted to visit, as in a museum, the objects I liked the most: a watch briefly seen during a visit to Antwerp, a solid gold crucifix, a Javanese scarf, whatever. I had become a kind of thief.

- And when do you start?

- It's done. You see me here as a spectral body while there, still a child, I have fun with my grandfather.

- My poor friend. It's going to be long.

- It's not so sure, you know. Time, still the time.

- What, it is faster in that life you are dreaming?

- It doesn't exist.

- What do you mean by that!

- It goes in all directions. Eternity. That's it. Eternity or cycles. Cycles in a loop. External whirlwind, internal whirlwind. A whole life revised.

- By whom?

-Well, by me of course! What do you think?

We heard the steps of three or four spiritualists going down the stairs. They were chatting away! Fervent words and, how should I say? Ecstatic, really, that's the word.

- *It is absolutely extraordinary. Our subject is incredible.*

- *Fantastic! Awfully exciting... It makes a change from the other.*

- *The other? Better forget about him, he was so dreary...*

- *Well, that's finished anyway... Never again. He made us lose so much time. What was he called? Flanders...*

They were talking about me.

- *This one is Belgian, like the other. Even more, he is a Belgian from Ghent, but what a difference!*

My creature was better than its creator, in a way.

- You'd think you were dreaming. They are talking about you.

- I will have to keep a close eye on that.

- Be careful! Perhaps your creature has decided to watch you closely. Perhaps it is actually inventing you.

- That's valid, you know? I imagined that Marian Poirier was a writer. A writer and a painter.

- Like you. Only more funny.

- Perhaps, but he has written a book. And in that book, he narrates my own life. With details I couldn't have made up. He couldn't have made up, I mean.

- That gives me food for thought...

- Well, earlier, I'm sure he was recounting my childhood. As if it was his... And of course, it's his, since I conceived a character that has devoted his life to following me everywhere. And what he was recounting is what he witnessed the day he arrived at my father's... With my sisters, Felicity and Nausicaa.

The echo of a voice interrupts me.

- Yes, I was there. Behind you. You couldn't see me. But I was there. Anyway, that's how I imagined the scene.

- Who's there?

- Poirier.

- Well well! Marian.

Nausicaa had a start. She looked around her, then she went down on all fours. She was calling someone.

- Marian?

- Marian? I know that name.

- Her cat. Hers, my cat doesn't have a name.

- A cat each?

- Don't be mistaken, my friend. It's the same cat. According to my sister, it's called Marian. I haven't found a name worthy of it yet. Worse: it shouldn't have a name. Under no circumstances. It would mean disobeying my father.

I went to inspect the place. Behind the sitting room, in which the previous scene took place, I discovered a tiny room.

Flanders' father was there.

- What are you doing here?

- I'm spying on you.

- So that's you! I was expecting you.

- What about you, what are you doing?

- I'm spying on my daughters.

- Your daughters and your son.

- Him? No! I don't feel like seeing him. You, on the contrary... With you, it's different, you are funnier.

- How do you know?

- Intuition.

- But I'm nothing but one of your son's inventions.

- That must be the reason I understand you better.

- I find you hard to follow... Patience. And you say you were expecting me?

- For approximately a week. I received a letter from your uncle Gaspard.

- In a way, your brother is the uncle of your son.

- It is not good being fussy like that, my dear friend. You say you are my son's invention, right?

- That seems to be the case...

- Then you are also my son. In the same way that I am, in a manner of speaking, the son of my own son.

- Why say that?

- Because I am aware of what he says about me. I have my informers, you know. Yes! I have certain mastery over time, which allows me to circulate freely in regions normally forbidden to simple minds. I am a master of time. A "little master", but a master nevertheless.

- You said "my informers"...

- Acquaintances, you know? People from another age.

- From the past…

- But we *are* in the past, my dear friend. I am well placed to know that. People say: "There is the past, the present and the future." But that's wrong… Or rather, it's right, but not necessarily in that order: we live in the future and spend our life travelling towards a past that we are forced to invent. And in that journey, we cross a turbulent region we can call the present. And on our return journey towards the future, we cross again the turbulent zone of the present. So we actually live twice, the journey towards the past and that of the return. Are you following me?

- I am not sure… According to you, we live our present twice?

- Not entirely, not entirely. The present is twofold, that's correct. But on each single and return journey, we modify both the future and the past. That's why the past and the future always seem to us hypothetical, and the storm we call the present, paradoxically more stable than the green region of the past and the red territories of the future.

He talked, and talked. And at each change of subject (I should have said "at each tremor"), we were forced to glide, to shift, to move away. From what? Good question. With no answer.

Example: the monologue that was embodied in the mouth of the master of time was saying:

- Here's how I see things, son: instability, because it repeats itself, because it insists, ends up settling, making itself visible, it accepts its plausibility with no false sense of propriety…

And here we are, facing the sea.

But this false reality breathes, sparkles, doesn't it? It palpitates. But it coughs, it sneezes, it is sometimes breathless.

And here we are suddenly facing a church.

This reality, in which we want to believe, sometimes generates desires, whims, impulses…

Then we find ourselves in an alleyway of a metallic grey, really revolting.

He keeps quiet. The décor becomes immutable, heavy. It is here to last.

But the clockmaker resumes his speech:

- ... impulses of infidelity. Yes, it exists, the infidelity of matter.

And here we are now climbing a staircase humid like an old man.

And the hundred-year-old walls, the castles, the impregnable fortresses, the ageless redouts...

It all becomes terribly whimsical, unstable. One doesn't know which way to turn.

And here we are in the studio of the master.

We looked at each other and it was the first time, I think, that we saw each other. For real. He was bald. "A skull, polished like a knee, surrounded by a thin halo of white hair that brought out even more the light pink tone of his skin."

Someone, not me, has just uttered these words.

- Is that how you see me? the master said. Well, you are mistaken, dear friend (or son or, why not, dear father). I am fit as a fiddle. I feel better than anyone else.

- But I said nothing.

- That's right, but you are thinking it, like everybody else in fact. Don't say anything, I know everybody thinks I'm dead and buried. But far from being dead, I feel better than anyone else. I am the most inspiring designer of clocks in the universe. In this very place, behind those shattered cupboards, you will discover cascades of glazed lampas, grotesque Chinese figurines, craquelure and celadon horns, cupids and nymphs in biscuit ware, Dresden china and old Sèvres porcelain. You are looking at that junk room, that bric-à-brac shop, and you say (you are already thinking it): "What is that old junk I can't make head or tail of?" Well, beware of appearances! These objects whose obsolescence, I know, is tickling you, are clocks. Nothing else. Only clocks. It is here that I try to tune the pulses of worldly things. And I'm not far from succeeding. Once that insane task is accomplished, we won't need time travel. It will be for worldly things to come to us now. Soon this will be the centre of the Universe. Of all the universes, actually.

- Actually?

He looks at me. And I have the feeling that he doesn't see me.

He smiles. To be honest, he is not looking at me. Not even. His eyes glide. He is flying over me like a migrating bird crossing the ocean.

A leaden silence makes our pneumatic bodies sink and we plunge vertiginously towards an unanimous sea.

Everything is falling. The so-called "bric-à-brac" turns around us at an almost military speed. It is parading, that's for sure. A kind of military march played by thousands of musical boxes harasses us with an almost sublime impertinence.

- What's happening to us? I say.

And my voice multiplies, scatters into a foaming sparkle.

Now I am alone. I am floating. Around me, the metallic acid blue sky breathes for me.

- Who's there?

There is no one around.

- Is there anybody there?

They are calling me. Finally! My dear spiritualists from the rue de Buci are coming to my rescue.

- I'm coming! I'm coming!

But what are those birds, suddenly appearing from all over, doing here? Why are they turning around me? And why do they proclaim with my voice: "I'm coming! I'm coming!"?

It looks like paper sheets on which one has stuck my image, repeated with a hardline care. Oddly enough, I am able to see those flying faces at the same time one by one and all together.

In reality, it is not that. Not exactly. Those flighty faces, I see them like multiple entities. Mutating. A real festival of grimacing faces, scattered in a pearly grey mass, a kind of cloud-mother. A whirlwind of cut-off heads (my heads) emerge from it, and already choke me, sticking to the extremely fragile surface of my astral body.

I am breathless!

Printed by
Petro Ofsetas
Lituania
EUROPE
november 2012